The three riders wheeled their horses and cantered them up the canyon.

Rance watched from the opening. "They're Comancheros!" He moved to the side, back of a boulder, and checked the loads in his carbine.

If they see this clearing and check it, he reminded himself, I can't let any of them get away, or I'll have a hundred men to fight. He sighed, rechecked the loads in his carbine and relaxed against a sun-warmed boulder until he heard the horses.

They rode into the clearing, three riders. Comancheros who were swarthy and mean, carrying carbines butted against their legs. They rode their horses slow, and the gunbelts that hung from their shoulders slashed across their bodies.

Rance felt the stabbing pain of his wound, but he ignored it as he cautiously watched the three riders.

The lead horseman saw the buckskin, swiveled in his saddle and discovered Rance.

As his eyes widened, Rance pointed his carbine and settled the front sight on his target.

LONG ROPER

Jim Wilmeth

TOWER BOOKS NEW YORK CITY

To Orpha, who fixes my grub and reads my books

A TOWER BOOK

Published by

Tower Publications, Inc.
Two Park Avenue
New York, N.Y. 10016

AUTHOR'S NOTE

In 1870, the time of this story, Texas was in the midst of reconstruction and carpetbag rule. The Texas Rangers had been disbanded for ten years, and the state's population of 800,000 lived almost wholly in that part of the state east and south of a line running from a point near the present day Wichita Falls south to San Antonio, then southwest to the Rio Grande River. West and north of that line was untamed country without organized counties and with only a scattering of frontier ranchers who had just moved into the Caprock country.

The Texas Panhandle, buttressed by the Caprock on the east, was the domain of the Plains Indians and the Comancheros who traded with them. The big Comanchero, Tafoya, with his band of men, traded at Tule Canyon. He and other Indian traders did business at Yellow House Canyon and Palo Duro Canyon.

East of the Caprock, frontier cattlemen such as H.M. Childress had a toehold in the Caprock country, and they forted themselves against raids by rustlers, mustangers, maverickers, Indians and occasionally Comancheros. Three years later, fed up with the rustling of his stock, Childress was to take a small group of his toughest cowhands, ride to New

Mexico Territory, and reposses every horse and cow carrying his brand. His counter raid was successful, but it did little to discourage the rustlers.

Against this backdrop of the Texas Frontier, I have drawn a picture of the violence of survival. Except for the obvious historical characters such as H.M. Childress, Tafoya the Comanchero, and places such as the relatively new Matador Ranch and the Caprock country, my characters are fictional but real in the sense of their attitudes and philosophies.

This story could and might have happened.

1

On a rocky bench in the Texas Caprock, Rance Long Roper had made a drifter's camp. Carefully hidden by head-high boulders and mesquite, he waited by a small fire for the sun. Jerky and coffee, he decided sourly, will stick to your ribs and warm you, but it's sure scant for a breakfast. The fire began to smoke, and he quickly adjusted the wood for a smoke-free fire.

He was dressed in throwouts and hand-me-downs of a drifter, and his trousers had begun to fray and his hat sagged wearily. Only his boots and gunbelt were newer and had escaped the wear of time. He raised a steaming cup of coffee to his lips and waited for the sun. The Caprock, he thought, has always been bushy tailed and onery mean, but it seems worse now. There's no Texas Rangers and five days ride to the nearest town marshal. Mr. Rath at Adobe Walls said that the Caprock is turning into a hellhole, he remembered. I sure can't argue that.

The sun edged above scrub oak hills and mesquite covered hogbacks. Rance slowly stood from his hunkered position by the fire, and as he warily studied the broken land below his camp, his buckskin mare snorted and shook the morning chill from her body. His eyes restlessly studied the country for rolls of dust that would warn him of mustangers.

Gaunt gutted and lean, he settled his weight, shifted the balance of a carbine in his hand and cautiously watched a dusty trail that ran north from Yellow House Canyon to Tule Creek and Palo Duro Canyon.

Tafoya's Comancheros are camped at Tule Canyon, he thought. That means for sure that mustangers will be running bands of horses up this trail. He shook his head sadly. "Why did I have to come down off the Panhandle when Tafoya is trading at Tule Canyon?" He smiled sourly. "There won't be a safe trail from here to the Matador Ranch." He contemplated his bedroll and camp gear. "It'd be nice to have a little ranch." He shook his head. "But that's not for the likes of me," he sighed.

The clearing warmed as it absorbed the sun's rays. It warmed his stiff muscles and he luxuriated in a smoke. A rattlesnake sluggishly worked its way across the rock-rubbled hillside below him, and as he listened, a bobwhite's whistle broke the silence. A coyote trotted onto the trail and settled on its haunches to enjoy the sun.

Over the early morning sounds, he could hear a rumbling that he knew was a band of horses.

Someone's running horses, he thought. It must be mustangers. No honest cowboy would do that. Moving away from the fire, he relaxed against a high boulder to watch. The coyote curiously watched the trail.

Horses rounded a turn in the trail behind an easy riding horseman. They frisked as they ran at a pace that would hold for several hours. The coyote slipped into the underbrush.

They sure look good, he thought, and smiled as he watched them. His smile vanished. Rance turned his head, tilted it and listened. Sounds of rifle fire rolled along the Caprock's walls from the south. Broken irregular sounds that punctuated the rumble of horses hoofs.

He hunkered beside the boulder and cradled the carbine in his arms where its worn bluing reflected the morning sun.

As Rance watched, his eyes narrowed, the boulder beside his head exploded with a ricochet, and he scrambled away from the opening.

"Dammit," he growled, "why are they shooting at me?" Crouch-walking to the fire, he grasped his saddle and blanket and ran to his horse. As he smoothed the blanket on his mare and settled the saddle on her back, he could hear a scrambling of horses on the hilly slope. Rocks tumbled and clattered. He whirled, scooped up his carbine and ran to the opening.

Two riders were halfway up the hillside. Rifle fire erupted from the horsemen below, and their bullets ripped a mesquite tree near him. A trunk shattered. Splinters of limbs showered him, as Rance settled beside the boulder and began firing. His bullets ricocheted from the loose sandstone and shale that littered the slope. They exploded the litter into dust. Rock fragments slashed at the riders.

The lead horseman reined back in panic. His horse

slid on a loose rock, lost its footing and rolled with its rider. He slipped his booted foot free of the stirrup, stepped from his saddle and scrambled to the shelter of a rocky outcropping.

The second rider reined his horse to a stop, dismounted and ran for the protection of a scrub oak. He tripped on a loose rock but scrambled out of sight.

The horse that had rolled came to its feet, shook itself and ambled down the slope with the second horse.

Rance settled himself and fired probing shots at the two men, searching for a good target. As he fired he reloaded from his gunbelt. Damn them, he thought. I'm getting tired of being shot at and chased everytime I make camp. It happened near Tascosa, at Running Water Draw, and now here.

The second man showed a spot of color through lacy branches of the scrub oak.

Rance's bullets ripped at the tree. Splinters and bark bits filled the air. He levered the carbine into a rolling sound that slashed at the rock rubble and the scrub oak.

The first man returned fire.

Rance's carbine swiveled and he levered shots at the man until it emptied to the hard sound of a snapping hammer. He began to reload.

The second man scrambled away from the scrub oak. He ran, fell and rolled down the hill.

Rance cursed himself for emptying the carbine. "Too damn far for a sixgun," he grumbled and began to thumb cartridges into the magazine.

The first man raced from his shelter and

scrambled down the slope.

Rance fired a single shot at the running man. Its ricochet sprayed rock dust in front of him, and as the men waiting on the trail watched, Rance turned back to his mare.

Down below Bart Ledbetter glowered at the two riders. "Dammit to hell," he growled as they legged into their saddles, "you can't even pry a drifter out of a clearing." His thick lips under a narrow beak of a nose sagged into a pout. "I told you to get him, and he run both of you off." He looked at the hillside and turned back to Billy Joe and Bob. "All of you, get your asses up there and get him before he gets away from the Caprock."

Rance led his buckskin along a game trail that skirted a dense growth of trees covering the hillside. Dammit, he thought, if I could get back onto the Panhandle I would. Getting to Dallas isn't that important. He paused and listened.

A flock of crows squawked angrily at an owl.

If they were so all fired anxious to come up the hill after me, they won't give up too easily. His buckskin snorted and he looked back at her. "What'd you hear, girl?" He paused, squatted and cautiously studied their backtrail and the trees that crowded in on them.

A brown sparrow deftly probed the loose bark of a scrub oak for a bug, and as he watched, the sparrow switched its tail at him and flew to another tree. A big rattlesnake, an eight-footer at least, raised its angular head from the trail and probed the air with its tongue before moving off the trail. It left a musty odor hanging in the air.

Rance shook his head. I don't like it, he thought. I've got a feeling about those mustangers. They were ready to kill me and now they're not around. He stood. "Let's go, girl." He pulled at the reins. "This game trail will take us onto the Panhandle or down to that trail. Either way is better than waiting here."

The mare turned her head and looked back at the trail.

Rance squatted and watched.

Two riders were cautiously working their way toward him.

Unbooting his carbine and easing himself around the mare, Rance jacked a cartridge into the chamber and called to them.

"Hello!" His greeting was abrupt and hard. "If you're looking for me, get the hell away." He fired a shot over their heads, turned and mounted.

The two men reined back suddenly as Rance nudged the mare into a canter.

"Get going, girl!" He spurred the buckskin into a run that carried them along a twisting trail between and around a jumble of boulders. They want me for some reason, he thought, but I don't aim to find out why.

As he topped a hill, Rance could see the two riders and they were gaining. The way my mare's loaded, he thought, I don't want to run her any more than I have to, but damn if I like to be pushed around and chased. He watched the backtrail. They're getting close. He gritted his teeth and kicked her into a run. They'll catch me if I don't do something.

The trail narrowed and threaded its way through

boulders and an outcropping of rock, down through a sluiceway and across a wide rocky saucer that was fractured and creviced. Beyond the saucer, it led over a shoulder of short grass and down into a mesquite thicket that crowded the trail.

Rance cantered his buckskin across the saucer and reined to a stop on the short grass. He spurred the mare and reined her back, wheeled her and stopped. Studying the tracks, he smiled thinly and patted the buckskin's neck.

"With the trail ahead being like it is, maybe they'll stop and consider." He walked her back onto the saucer to a cluster of boulders where he tied her out of sight. Now I'll find a place to wait, he decided.

Billy Joe and Bob watched the trail as they rode onto the rocky saucer. Their horses were wind weary and saddle sore, and flecks of blood beaded around spur-scarred flanks.

"I don't like this." Bob shook his head. "A bushwhacker could lay out and get a sight on us anytime he wants."

"I feel naked."

"The best thing is to get across as soon as we can," Bob suggested.

"Let's go."

They nudged their tired horses into a canter and slowed as they reached the short grass.

"Wait." Billy Joe raised his hand. He pointed to the chewed-up grass.

"What do you make of it, Billy Joe?"

"Looks like he's maybe figuring to bushwhack us."

"That mesquite thicket would be good for that."

"Then why'd he mess up this grass?"

"I sure don't know." Bob stood in his saddle and studied the mesquite thicket, settled back and shook his head. "I sure don't know."

"Let's go back where it's safe and do some figuring."

"I don't like to set out in the open."

"Maybe he messed up this grass so that we'd stop and he could get a sight on us."

"Maybe that's it." Bob wheeled his horse away from the short grass.

As they reined to a stop on the rocky saucer, Rance's mare whinnied.

"Where'd that come from?"

"Yonder." Bob pointed.

"Where would he be?" Billy Joe's voice was low. "I don't like the idea of—"

"Look behind you," Rance's voice interrupted.

They swiveled in their saddles as Rance stepped from a shallow crevice where he had hidden. The carbine moved restlessly, searching for a target.

"Wait," Billy Joe urged. His smile was weak. "You ain't the man we want."

"That's your mistake," Rance said dryly. "Shuck your gunbelts." His words were blunt and hard.

Billy Joe slowly lowered his right hand.

"Left hand!" Rance ordered abruptly.

He changed hands, unbuckled and let his gunbelt drop where it clattered beside his horse's hoofs.

"You." Rance pointed the carbine at Bob. "Unbuckle!" He gestured with the carbine. "Now!"

Bob slowly lowered his left hand. He paused and studied Rance.

14

"I've had an itch all the way from my camp to pay somebody back for being chased," Rance warned.

"You got us wrong," Billy Joe interrupted. "Let me tell you what happened."

"You'll be telling people how your partner was killed, if he doesn't drop that belt."

Bob unbuckled and let the gunbelt drop. It clattered on the rocky flat.

"Now both of you step down slow and move over there." Rance motioned with the carbine.

Billy Joe swung down and turned. His head tilted and he studied Rance. "We told you we figured you was someone else."

"Yeah, you did."

"Then why in the hell are you taking our guns?" His shoulders tensed and hunched forward.

"It ain't right what you're doing," Bob added as he dismounted and turned to face Rance.

"Ain't that a shame." Rance shifted his weight but held the carbine steady.

"Are you going to keep our guns?" Billy Joe grunted the question.

"For now."

His body squatted, his eyes squinted, and his mouth drew down. "Nobody's done that before." The corners of his mouth quivered. "And you ain't going to."

Rance settled on his feet and waited. "I don't want to kill you."

Bob watched his brother. His eyes narrowed. "Billy Joe, you calm down." He moved toward him.

Billy Joe's bowed legs began to pump as he charged at Rance. Boots scraped on the rocky flat, and his spurs rang as Billy Joe's mouth opened with a roar.

Rance shifted to the side.

Billy Joe swerved with him. His foot slipped, he stumbled but kept his footing.

Reversing his carbine, Rance slashed with the butt.

It made a hard cracking sound as Billy Joe charged past Rance, sprawled on the rock and slid into a grotesque heap.

Rance pointed the carbine at Bob as he backed around to look at the crumpled man.

"Is he dead?" Bob tilted his head anxiously.

"No. He's breathing."

Billy Joe moved and groggily sat up. "You ain't going to keep our guns," he growled and pushed himself to his knees. He shook his head and glared at Rance.

Rance's eyes flicked to Bob and back to the crouching man.

Bob squatted and glanced at their guns.

He saw Bob's interest in the guns as Billy Joe raised himself on one knee. Stepping toward Billy Joe, Rance kicked.

Billy Joe tried to dodge the boot, but it opened his cheek from jaw to temple.

Bob lunged for the guns.

Rance whirled and fired as the carbine swung to point.

His bullet ricocheted near Bob as he reached for his sixgun. He levered three rounds that threw up a cloud of dust near the guns.

Bob rolled away. "No! Don't!" he called.

Their horses reared and trotted away.

Billy Joe lay sprawled on the rocky flat, and Bob sat dejectedly as he watched Rance collect the two guns and walk to their horses.

He turned to Bob and smiled sadly. "I'm a peaceable man, but I don't take kindly to people following me. When your partner comes to, you can start walking. You'll find your horses and guns on the way to Dallas."

Rance cautiously threaded his way through a mesquite thicket and studied the trail to Palo Duro Canyon. Only a dust devil bounced and swirled a loose dusting of sandy loam. A coyote slipped onto the trail, studied both directions and began to roll in the dust.

The coyote thinks it's safe, he thought. That's good enough for me. He led the buckskin onto the trail and legged himself into the saddle.

The coyote gave Rance a startled glance and darted up the trail, attempted to swerve into the undergrowth and trees, but skidded, slid and rolled on the trail. The coyote scrambled to its feet and disappeared into the trees.

Four horsemen had startled the coyote when they rode out of a clearing they were checking. One of the men saw Rance.

"There he is!"

Rance heard the man, swiveled in his saddle and lay his spurs into the flanks of the buckskin.

The four riders spurred their horses.

Lashing the buckskin, Rance kicked her into a run toward a trail he'd used before. If I don't get to that trail, he thought, they'll catch me.

The riders slowed their horses.

Rance drew away and smiled grimly. His smile vanished.

Two mounted men were waiting on the trail, carbines leveled.

Thick growths of mesquite lined the trail and he slowed the mare. "Dammit," he growled and reined to a stop. He settled back in his saddle and watched the riders. No way out, he decided. His body was tensed and a bead of perspiration edged itself down his back.

The four riders cantered toward him, slowed and reined to a step. A tall rider grinned a lopsided smile and spit a stream of tobacco juice to the trail. He wiped his mouth with a sleeve.

"Looks like we got him, Vache."

"Yep." Vache Green studied Rance's saddle and smiled sadly. "I figured he'd have a better saddle. It ain't no better than mine."

"You can worry about that later." He turned to Rance as the other riders reined to a stop beside them. "Mister, it looks like you rustled the wrong horses." He pointed to Billy Joe and Bob's horses. "Maybe we got you for murder. Ain't that what they call killing a man?" He grinned at Vache.

"They're all right," Rance said. "You'll find them on the trail back a ways."

"I'll go find them," a rider offered. "Let me have their horses, and don't do anything till I get back."

As Rance watched, Vache Green gestured to the tall rider. "High Pockets, help him down."

High Pockets swung his carbine like a club.

Rance felt the jarring crush of the carbine against

18

his back. He swayed forward and rolled. Reeling out of his saddle, Rance stumbled and sprawled on the trail. Rolling to his feet, he moved to the side.

The riders spurred their horses toward him. Trail dust swirled around them.

The sixgun that appeared in Rance's hand pointed, but he held his fire. He moved to the side of Vache's horse.

As Vache swung to point his carbine, Rance slashed at the horse's flank with the barrel of his sixgun and yelled.

"Eyahaa!"

Vache's horse broke into his aim. It arched its back and ruined his shot.

Rance swiveled and began firing. He fired as he moved in the dust that hung and drifted in the air.

Nervous tired horses whinnied and jumped half-bucks.

A man rolled out of his saddle. His horse, wide-eyed and throwing its head, collided with two mounted men and their horses.

Rance fanned his last two shots, wheeled to his buckskin, and as his booted foot slipped into the stirrup, he slapped the mare with his free hand.

She jumped into a run that swung Rance into his saddle. "Eyahaa! Let's go."

A trail he had used on his last trip angled east through a jumble of rock. It caused him to slow the buckskin. This will take me north of the Matador Ranch and on to Dallas, he thought. It'll get me out of this damm place.

2

"It ain't easy, Mr. Ledbetter," Bob Canutt argued and looked at his brother. "Billy Joe and me ain't anxious to die chasing some drifter." He absent-mindedly scratched his neck.

"He knows how to use his carbine," Billy Joe added.

"Cleaned our plows for sure," Vache Green said.

High Pockets spit. "It's hard to judge. You can't get good shooting when you're straddling a horse."

"And you said kill him. What's wrong with just letting him leave the country?" Bob continued. He produced a strip of jerky and chewed on it as he watched Ledbetter from the corner of his eye.

"He's mean for sure," High Pockets said. "Best you keep that in mind."

"I don't want him or anyone else getting away from the Caprock before Tafoya moves. I don't give a damm how mean he is." He nodded and glared at Bob. "Killing that cowboy this morning was a damm fool thing to do. It could warn every rancher that Tafoya is going to raid into Texas."

"Who cares?" Billy Joe grunted. "We could kill that drifter and bury him in some ravine. No one'll know the difference and Tafoya could still make the raid."

"That's what I want, as long as the ranchers don't find out," Ledbetter snapped. "Two more years and I'm going back to Washington in style. I've got plans, and I'm not going to let some stupid killing ruin five years of work."

"What's wrong with killing a drifter away from the Caprock?" High Pockets slouched in his saddle, his mouth sagged open from a plug of tobacco in his jaw, and he watched Bart curiously. "Maybe you ain't as mean as you're putting on."

Bart's mustang wheeled as he drew his sixgun in a cross draw and leveled it at High Pockets. "I'm not paying you for maybe this or that. Since you want to know how mean I can be, crawl off that horse."

High Pockets eyes widened. He spit out his chaw of tobacco and wiped his arm against the tobacco on his jaw. "You ain't man enough—"

The hard metallic cocking of Bart's sixgun interrupted the tall man.

"Look, I—" he reasoned.

"Unbuckle your gunbelt and crawl off that horse pronto."

High Pockets cautiously eased his leg over the cantle and lowered himself to the ground. "Mr. Ledbetter, I didn't—"

"Unbuckle. Now!"

His gunbelt dropped.

"Now take your hat off in my presence, walk over here and kiss my boot."

High Pockets back stiffened and he glared at Bart.

21

Bart's sixgun pointed, he cleared his throat and spit. "At this distance, I can put a bullet right between your eyes."

His shoulders sagged, he removed his hat and walked to Bart.

As High Pockets bent to kiss Bart's boot, Ledbetter reached for his hair and gripped it in his hand, slipped his boot foot from the stirrup and kicked.

High Pocket's nose and cheekbone collapsed. Blood cascaded down his face and across his shirt front.

Bart swung his booted foot around and raked the tall man's back with his spur.

He staggered away from Bart and stumbled as Ledbetter slid from his saddle. Bart held his gun raised as he dropped to the ground. It flashed in a short arc and left a bloody gash across High Pocket's head.

He staggered back.

Bart kicked.

He twisted, sagged and collapsed into a heap.

Bart's grin was twisted as he holstered his gun and turned to the watching men. "There's a hell of a lot of money to be got out here." He walked to his horse. "High Pockets might try to kill me. If he does, you'll all lose." He legged into his saddle and looked down at the bloodied man. "There's a hundred dollars for the man who kills him if he tries."

The riders watched High Pockets stand, walk to his horse and leg himself into the saddle.

"What do you want us to do about the drifter?" Billy Joe asked.

"You get him and kill him before he gets away."

"Even if he gets out of the Caprock?"

"That's what I said, and you come back with his scalp. I'll be at Tule Canyon."

Rance could smell wood smoke before he came onto the flat where he saw a cluster of shanties and a store. By the side of one of the shanties, in a haphazardly built corral that sagged at a corner, a blaze-faced dun and a sorrowfully colored burro curiously watched him rein his buckskin to the hitching rail.

He carefully studied the clearing before swinging to the ground. No horses, he thought. Only the dun and burro in the corral. No saddles, no gear. He studied the sandy loam of the clearing. Tracks are a day old anyway. He nodded and stepped down from his saddle.

"Are you going to wait there all day or come in and visit?"

The voice he heard came from a large woman who bulked in the doorway of the store and saloon. It sounded brusque and slightly hoarse. A voice accustomed to calling to a rider across a canyon or hogs in a cedar brake. His eyes widened momentarily as he looked at her. He swallowed and nodded.

"Door's open, come on in," she said and turned back into the store.

He stretched the stiffness in his back, and after brushing trail dust from his pants, walked to the store. As he paused in the doorway, then crossed the room to a counter that ran along the back wall, he studied her.

"Doggone, this is a big bar. I thought it was just a store." He turned his head and looked at the kerosene lamps that hung from the rafters.

"It gets full on Saturday nights. On payday I need more room." She stood against the backbar, arms folded across her breasts. Her hair was drawn tight against her head and rolled into a bun at the back, and her ankle-length dress was tie-stringed closed at her throat. "You want something or just to visit? Take your choice. I've got enough of whatever it is you need, jerky or pinole, whiskey or food."

"I could sure use some food."

"Well, I've got chili and beans or bootheel beef."

"Tough?"

"Tough as whang leather."

"Chili and beans would be good." He laughed. "And biscuits, if you've got 'em."

"I sure do. I'm proud of my biscuits. I cook them with pure hog lard and they're plain good."

"And maybe a little whiskey while I'm waiting."

He rested his arms on the counter and toyed with his drink as she returned with a large bowl of chili and a heaping platter of biscuits.

"You look familiar, like someone I know or maybe heard of." She watched him from the corner of her eyes as she wiped the counter with a tattered towel.

"Yes, ma'am," he answered between bites of food. "This sure is good. I like these biscuits."

She smiled. "Is your name Wes Hardin?"

He swallowed suddenly, looked at her and shook his head. "No, ma'am, I sure ain't."

"Well, I'm Laura Green, and if you ain't Wes Hardin, I'm sorry. His description fits you, and they say he's up around these parts. I'd sure like to meet him." She laughed suddenly. "If I could say Wes Hardin stopped by, I'd have more business than I could use." She looked at him with a sly smile. "You sure you ain't Wes Hardin?"

"No, ma'am," he laughed. "My name's Rance Long Roper."

"Not Wes?" She sounded disappointed.

He shook his head.

"Long Roper?" Laura turned to face him. "I've heard stories about you."

"Everywhere I go, someone's heard stories that ain't true," he complained.

"There was a shooting at Dodge."

"I was there, just resting on the street. Someone started shooting and I scooted down an alley." His laugh was quiet. "I don't know who was shooting or why."

"What about robbing a bank at Medicine Lodge?"

"That was a mistake," he argued. "A crooked banker sole me some land that wasn't his, and I went back to get my money."

"What happened?"

"Well, he didn't want to give me the money, so I busted up some furniture and his nose to boot. I got my money and then got out of town ahead of the sheriff."

She smiled, giggled and began to laugh. Walking to the end of the bar, she turned, still laughing, and wiped her eyes. "I'd like to have seen that." Laura brought a bottle down the counter. "That deserves a drink." She poured. "With your name, everyone figures the stories are true."

"Long Roper," he agreed, "makes you think of maverickers and rustlers, but my mother's name was Long. She took good care of me because my dad ran out on us when I was about a year old." His eyes saddened and he looked at his whiskey. "I aim to keep the name."

Laura glanced away. "I'm sorry."

"Thank you, ma'am." He sighed. "She went to rest in fifty-five and I started drifting. Fifteen years I've drifted and guess I always will." He looked up. "Fact is, you look enough like mom to be her sister."

She smiled and nodded. Her eyes saddened and she looked away. "Consumption?"

"Yes, ma'am."

"A lot of good people have died of consumption."

"It hits everyone," he agreed. "Missus Green, is there any land around here that a poor old cowboy could pick up reasonable like?"

She rested an elbow on the counter and smoothed her hair. "Most of the land has been taken. The Matador is only a half a day's ride south, and Childress is feeding his cattle in most of the canyons and ravines north of here. There are good people here. Childress, Garvey and a lot of others are almost like family, but it's land poor. South of the Matador, it's mostly rock, sand, cockle burrs and rattlers." She sighed. "It's poor picking if you're looking for land." She paused and tilted her head. "Riders, hear them?"

Rance straightened, turned and moved to a window of greased deer hide that hung half open.

Laura walked to the door. She waved to a group of horsemen as they rode by.

"We'll be back," a rider called.

"They're a part of the Matador bunch," she said and turned away from the door. She paused and watched Rance holster the sixgun he had drawn.

"Just cautious," he said and walked back to his drink.

"Is someone after you?"

"No, ma'am. I had a run in with some mustangers this morning because of a misunderstanding. There was some shooting."

"A sixgun is a strong convincer in a misunderstanding." She ladled more chili and beans into his bowl. "Have some more biscuits."

"Whewee, this is good." His face saddened. "Mom made biscuits like these."

She nodded.

"Drifting like I've been," he said, "I've had more trouble than biscuits, and all I want is to settle down."

"You don't have to be a drifter to have troubles. Texas has its share, and reconstruction hasn't helped, what with the carpetbaggers up here."

"This part of Texas, carpetbaggers?"

She nodded. "Bart Ledbetter's trying to get control of all of the land in this part of the country and maybe squeeze out the Matador, Childress and the other ranchers." She shook her head. "He's no good. Some say he's tied in with Tafoya."

Rance nodded and tilted his head. "Riders?"

She nodded.

The sounds of running horses came loud.

Rance stepped away from the counter as Laura moved around the bar. She shook her head. "Put that gun away or they'll kill you."

He paused as the sounds of horsemen and horses filled the room. Bootheels and spur rowels preceded a man who walked through the door.

"Garvey. Howdy."

"Howdy, Missus Laura." He turned slowly and studied Rance. "We're looking for some men who killed one of my cowboys this morning."

"Where did it happen?" She moved back of the counter.

"North of Yellow House." He continued to study Rance. "Are you drifting?"

Rance nodded. "I came off the Caprock above Running Water Draw."

"Did you see anyone?"

He nodded. "Mustangers, I figure. They were heading north with about fifty head of horses."

Garvey nodded. "They were my horses." He turned and looked at Rance's buckskin. "Is that your horse with the stocking rear feet?"

"Yes, sir."

"Red." He motioned. "You saw the men who took my horses?"

"Yes, sir, I did."

"That buckskin with the stocking rear feet. Have you seen it before?"

3

Rance eased himself to the window and watched a cowboy lean forward and study the buckskin.

Red shook his head. "I don't think so, Mr. Garvey. No buckskin or stocking feet. I ain't sure, but I don't think so."

Rance slowly relaxed.

"Red says he don't think so, and I'll stand by that. If I find out," he warned, "that you're riding with them, I'll find you and hang you from the nearest tree." He wheeled and walked out.

Laura looked at Rance and gestured with her head. "He just lost a cowboy. Why don't you hit him up for a job?"

"With my name?" His smile was sour. "That's all he'd need to get his justice," he said bitterly. "Who cares about a drifter when they can hang him for a killer?"

"If you don't, no one else will."

He nodded and smiled thinly. "All right." Rance walked to the door. "Mr. Garvey, can I talk to you?"

Garvey turned as Rance appeared in the door.

"I'm looking for a job."

Garvey grunted sourly, tilted his head and

studied Rance. "You want a job?"

"I sure do."

"Why should I hire you?"

"You need a rider."

"I hired a man to take care of my horses. He was killed and they were stolen."

"How about ranch work?"

"I've got my men."

"I know cattle. I'm good at branding and as good a roper as you've got."

"If you're that good, why are you looking for work?"

"It gets cold up in Kansas."

Garvey smiled. "What's your name?"

Rance paused and took a breath. "Rance Long Roper."

His smile disappeared. "Long Roper?"

"Yes, sir."

One of the riders grunted. "Owlhooter."

"I'll give you an honest day's work."

"We've heard stories about you and most of them are probably wrong, but maybe some are true." Garvey scratched his neck and looked at Rance. "Tell you what I'll do."

Rance relaxed.

"You might be able to help me, especially if the stories about you are half true. I'll hire you for a month and see how it works out. If you do a good job, I'll hire you on regular."

"Thank you, sir."

"I'm not through. Your job's to get my horses back, pure and simple."

Rance laughed sourly. "They'll be in New Mexico

30

by tonight."

"Maybe not." Garvey swung into his saddle. "We'll be back by here in a while. If you want the job, be ready to ride."

Rance and Laura had waited.

Garvey's riders followed him into the room. He bellied up to the counter beside Rance. "All right." He turned to face Rance. "Do you want the job?"

Rance nodded. "I've figured a way to get your horses back, but I'll need help."

"I don't want any of my men killed."

"Not that. I want some catch men to corral a stampeding bunch of horses."

A young cowboy studied Rance. "If you figure on going into that camp, you'll need a lot of help." He glanced at Garvey and back at Rance.

"No." Rance rubbed his hands and studied his whiskey. "If there's any shooting, I don't want to worry about who's on who's side."

"Hell, he must have a hundred men in camp."

"That's right. Mustangers, Indians, and Comancheros. It'll be early in the morning, they'll be half asleep, and who ever heard of Tafoya getting his stock stolen? They won't expect that to happen."

"You're loco."

"You may be right, but that's the way I'm going to do it." He turned to Garvey. "What will you pay?"

"I'm paying my men twenty dollars a month and keep. That's better than a lot of ranches. I'll pay twenty and a fifth of what you recover."

"There'll be a passel of horses."

"Most of the other ranchers will give you a fifth."

"All right, that's a deal." Rance turned to Garvey's cowboys. "Do any of you know the trails that will get me into Tule Canyon?"

Rance slowed the buckskin and stepped down from his saddle. He led his mare and cautiously probed each turn in the torturous trail that wound haphazardly into the canyon. Dark clouds hung above the Caprock and he could hear a distant rumble of thunder. The sun's rays brightened the canyon's high rising walls, and it would soon lighten the dark shadows of the trail he was following. He could smell rain and the air felt heavy and damp. A coyote sang its song to the sun, and an owl launched itself for a final hunt.

When the sun hits that trail, he thought, I'll have thirty minutes before Mr. Garvey and his men start riding, and if that's a cloudbuster hanging over the Caprock, I'll have an hour to get the hell out of the canyon.

The early morning sounds of Tafoya's Comancheros saddling their horses drifted along the trail and echoed from the canyon walls. He cautiously raised himself on a stirrup and studied the canyon. Rolls of dust drifted in the air where it caught the sun's early light.

This trail will take me into the canyon, he thought, and back of Tafoya's camp. His smile was slight. I'll have to bust them horses out, right through the camp. He shook his head. I'll have to spook them for sure before they'll stampede, but most of them are rustled stock so they're a mite edgy. He crouched and studied a turn in the trail. If they don't stampede, Tafoya will corral them and his Indians will sure as hell track me down. He considered the odds, shook his head sadly and watched dark shadows on the trail lighten.

The dim figure of a trail guard, hidden in the predawn shadows, was suddenly silhouetted against a brightly lighted canyon wall.

Rance watched him stretch the stiffness from his back and relax against a boulder.

"Damn," he growled under his breath. "I haven't got much time before Mr. Garvey'll be starting up the trail." He eased his buckskin to the side of the trail and squatted beside a mesquite.

What had been the sounds of milling horses became a babble of voices. The sun's light reflected by a mirror on the canyon wall flashed. The voices were angry, excited and profane. The mirror flashed wildly and Rance looked up at a tiny figure on the canyon rim. He could see a serape-draped man gesturing to the south. "Garvey's on the way," he grunted and moved to study the trail guard. He heard the man's horse snort, the creak of saddle leather and the pounding run of the guard's horse that faded into the yells and uproar of the Comancheros.

Rance led his buckskin mare into a hidden clearing where he eased the cinch.

"Now you keep quiet," he ordered and turned away.

She snorted.

33

He followed the trail along a canyon wall where he could see the confused Comanchero camp. "Garvey sure got them all excited. I don't think that's ever happened to them before." He grinned broadly and squatted beside a boulder to watch.

The Comancheros ignored the clearing as they watched the approach of Garvey and his men.

Unholstering his Walker Colt, Rance inspected the percussion caps on its cylinder and replaced one. "I'm going to have to get new nipples on that cylinder or a new gun," he grumbled. "They tell me there's a Smith and Wesson that shoots a forty-four. Just like my carbine." He grinned. "That'd be slick." He slipped the Walker into its holster, latched it down and turned his attention to the camp.

The confusion and noise had disappeared and Tafoya's camp seemed empty and deserted. Dust hung in the air like thin layers of clouds and it drifted with the breeze. Long shadows of the morning sun lay across the camp, where an occasional raider crossed the clearing.

"Dammit," he growled, "where'd they go?"

Horses milled uneasily in a corral between Rance and the camp, and a hundred yards up the canyon, a picketline fence held a larger bunch. They whinnied nervously.

Rance turned his head to study the second corral. The horses stood bunched watching the camp. I don't see a soul, he thought. Garvey must be putting on a big show. He grinned happily. I wanted him to attract their attention. I didn't figure the whole camp would hide out and wait for him.

He stood, balanced his carbine and crouch-ran to the corral near the camp. The horses turned and watched as he threaded himself between the railings. A buckskin and dun shied as he walked into the bunch.

Rance rubbed the neck of a mare and began to walk her toward two railings that were used as a gate. He stopped when he heard a voice. A sense of danger that he could almost smell began to itch his scalp.

A man called from the camp.

Through the loosely milling horses, Rance saw him cross the clearing to his horse.

The man legged into his saddle, wheeled his horse and rode to the corral.

Crouched against the mare, Rance could feel perspiration bead between his shoulder blades, and his back muscles tensed as he watched.

The rider turned and called. "Zeke, get your ass down here and stop worrying about them riders on the trail." He waved to a second rider.

"What the hell do you want?" He reined up and stopped beside the first rider.

"Tafoya don't want to lose these horses and I don't aim to be at fault if someone sneaks in the back way."

"You worry too much." The second man laughed. "The lookout will spot anyone that tries that. He can see every trail leading into Tule. Let's check the other corral."

Rance continued to work his mare through the horses as both men rode to the second corral. The mare became nervous as she neared the gate railings. He slowed and cautiously studied the empty camp. "They sure disappeared," he said quietly and patted the mare's neck. "As long as they keep watching Mr. Garvey and his cowboys, I don't care."

She snorted and calmed.

Rance reached for the railings and moved them just enough that they would drop with a push. "That's done. Now I'll get acros the corral and figure what to do next."

Lightning slashed at a dark line of clouds that hung above the Caprock. It speared across the sky and lighted a heavy roll of thunderheads.

The mare nervously jumped and nickered.

Thunder rolled across the canyon as the two riders returned to camp.

As he watched, they disappeared around an outcropping of the canyon wall. The horse band began to mill and a few shook their heads. They're getting spooky, he thought. Maybe I can break those horses out of the other corral and all of them will stampede. He grinned at the mare and rubbed her neck. His smile vanished as he felt the heavy drops of rain. A light flurry raised puffs of dust in the corral.

"I've got to move," he grunted, "or a gully washer could clean this whole canyon out."

The lookout signaled wildly with the mirror.

Rance legged through the corral fence and ran to the second corral. He was afraid to look at the camp. "The lookout might have spotted me."

The wind gusted and blew dust in his face as he dropped the gate railings of the corral. It's going to rain like hell. I've got to move, he thought. My luck's been too good to last. He looked up at the clouds.

As the railings dropped, the two riders returned and saw Rance. They spurred their horses into a run. Rifle fire erupted from the camp. A bullet ricocheted from the corral fence. A horse whinnied and shook its head.

He skirted the edgy band of horses and, as the riders neared the corral, pointed his carbine at the sky and began firing. As his three shots racketed in the canyon, Rance raised his voice. "Eyahaa!"

The riders reined to a stop as the horse band spooked. They wheeled their horses to the side.

"Eyahaa!"

The horses stampeded out of the corral.

The two riders began firing at Rance.

Horses streamed out of the corral as thunder exploded near the head of the canyon.

He lowered the carbine and, as Zeke thumbed his sixgun, Rance sighted and fired.

Zeke's body twisted back against the cantle. He grasped the horn of his saddle and, as his horse wheeled, dropped his gun.

Zeke's partner reined away from the stampeding horses, raised his gun and tried to get a sight on Rance, but his horse tossed its head and attempted to turn.

Rance ran along a trail between the corral and canyon wall and slipped out of sight behind a jumble of boulders.

Thunder crashed across the canyon. As he watched, the horses in the first corral panicked and crashed through the gate railings that had been loosened.

The two horse bands merged and pounded through the Comanchero camp.

Tafoya's men erupted from the hillside and the trees that lined the trail.

The horse band dodged but they followed a blaze-faced sorrel that had become their leader.

"All right, Mr. Garvey," Rance mumbled under his breath, "your horses are on the way." He trotted along the trail back to his buckskin.

Bob and Billy Joe Canutt saw Rance as he followed a winding trail, and they waited on their horses at a turn in the trail.

"What are you going to do?" Bob asked.

"I'm going to kill him. Ledbetter and Tofoya will like that." Billy Joe hunkered in his saddle and waited.

Rance looked at the low hanging clouds as the rain steadied. It soaked through his jacket and pants. He felt it along his backbone, and rainwater standing on the trail splashed as he walked.

Rain in the canyon pounded into a roar.

The rain sheeted and swirled in his face. It's been raining on the Panhandle, he thought. That roar must be the run off. He paused as he heard a voice.

"Hold it," Bob ordered.

Rance looked up and saw the two riders.

"Now you stand still," Bob said.

Billy Joe grinned and pointed his sixgun.

Thunder rumbled in the distance.

Rain spilled from his hat as Rance looked at the two men.

Their horses nervously tossed their heads.

"Shuck your gun," he ordered.

Rance's eyes widened momentarily, his muscles tensed and he eased his body into a squat.

Billy Joe thumbed the hammer of his sixgun.

"No!" Bob moved his hand to Billy Joe. "I've got an idea." They glanced at each other.

The sheeting rain swirled around them as lightning speared the sky.

Rance swung the carbine, pointed and its exploding sound ripped the dimness with a stabbing muzzle flash.

As their frightened horses reared, Bob and Billy Joe began firing.

Rance dived for the shelter of a boulder. He felt the hot jolting pain of a bullet in his side. Ricochets sprayed him with gravel, dirt and rock fragments.

"Get him," Billy Joe roared.

Bob spurred his horse toward the boulder.

Rance swung the carbine to point and levered three fast rounds.

A bullet creased Bob's shoulder. He swayed to the side and dropped his gun.

Rance swiveled his carbine toward Billy Joe and lashed the dimness with the angry flash of gunfire.

Their horses panicked, reared and half-bucked.

They tried to hold the frightened horses but their hands slipped on wet reins, and the horses raced away.

"Dammit," Rance grunted and probed the wound with his fingers. "It feels bad, but maybe I can make it." He looked up the trail. "I've got to get out of here, or they'll bring Tafoya and all of his men down on my back." He wheeled and trotted to the clearing where his buckskin waited.

The buckskin snorted as he entered the clearing. Rance raised his hand to her nostrils. "Easy girl. They're looking for me." As he cinched the saddle down, he could feel the blood force its way past a scab that had begun to form. He paused, then slowly drew the cinch tight.

I don't have much time to get out of here before every trail will be flooded, he decided, and I've got to find somewhere to hole up where Tafoya can't find me. Laura Green's place is too far. He grinned sourly and nodded. There's a buffalo hunter's dugout in Palo Duro.

4

A crash of thunder bounced its sounds against the walls of Tule Canyon. A sprinkle of rain died away as the storm moved to the east, the clouds began to break up, and a blue sky overhead gave a sparkle to the rain-soaked canyon.

Tafoya walked onto the trail, glared at his men and turned slowly as he studied them. His mouth drew into a hard thin line. "Bastard sons of the whores you call mother! You are no better than the gringo pigs who stole my horses." He turned on his heel and lumbered angrily toward his camp. "Sanchez, Raoul! A fire pronto!"

His Comancheros followed sheepishly. They straggled along, booted feet splashing in the muddy rainwater, and hesitantly formed a ring around Tafoya. Gunbelts hung from their shoulders over unkempt clothing that was worn and tattered. With emotionless faces and cold eyes, they waited as Sanchez and Raoul started a fire.

Renegade Apache and Yaqui Indians, mustangers and rustlers waited with Ledbetter and his men as Tafoya angrily damned them all.

"Senor Ledbetter," Tafoya turned to the carpetbagger, "your men know this country?" He gestured to the east. "They know the trails and ranches?"

"They sure do."

"Bueno. You will guide us."

"I ain't sure—"

"My horses were stolen," he interrupted. Tafoya's eyes hardened beneath his bushy eyebrows. "You will, or you are not my amigo," he said flatly. "You said you want to work with me. Now you are not sure."

The Comancheros turned to watch Ledbetter. They shifted their feet restlessly. A Comanchero jacked a cartridge into his carbine and glowered at him.

"The trails are narrow and winding," Bart explained. "They'd know you were coming before you got five miles on the trail."

Tafoya turned and studied the rough broken country. He nodded and turned back to the fire that had flamed up. "Si, they would." He turned to Bart. "My horses. What will they do with them?"

"There's not much chance of getting them back," Billy Joe interrupted. "By morning they'll be scattered in every ravine and gully for fifty miles, and there ain't enough daylight left to catch them before they're scattered."

Tafoya shrugged and shook his head. "The gringo who stole them. Where will he be?" His mouth drew into an angry line as he thought of Rance.

"It's hard to know where he is," Billy Joe answered, "but we can find him."

Tafoya grinned evilly. "Kill him if you have to, but I'll pay you double if you bring him to me alive."

"How much are you paying?"

"My Comancheros do not ask," he snapped angrily.

"I'm asking."

"Bring him to me and we will talk." He turned to a Comanchero named Perez, spoke to him in border Spanish and gestured to the north.

Perez nodded and motioned to two other men. They walked to their saddled horses and mounted.

Billy Joe glanced curiously at Bob and returned his attention to Tafoya.

"They will search the canyon." Tafoya began to roll a cigarette. "You will go and find him pronto." He lighted the cigarette and turned to Ledbetter. "The gringo rancher Childress, he has many horses, you say."

"And cattle," Bart added.

"You want to raid?"

"With you. We know the trails and you have the men."

"We will talk later." He turned to his Comancheros and motioned for a bottle of whiskey.

The sun broke through rain clouds and shined on the grass and sandy flood plain of Palo Duro. Rance slowed his buckskin and studied a cluster of house-high boulders for the narrow opening to a trail that would take him to the dugout. He had circled a herd of buffalo on the broad grassy flood plain, and he could still smell them. They'll move back up the canyon, he thought, and cover my tracks. He reined to a stop when he saw the opening, nodded and grinned. The dugout looked deserted. Its door hung half open and bunch grass grew around the doorway.

Reining his buckskin along a trail that threaded itself between boulders and into a small clearing in front of the dugout, Rance dismounted. The saddle dropped as he loosened the cinch. He let it lay, released the mare and walked slowly to the dugout with his bedroll.

The pint bottle of whiskey he had carried all the way from Dodge City felt good on the wound and tasted better in his gut. It burned all the way down and warmed him. Just in case, he grinned, and raised the bottle again. Bandaged and smeared with ointment, he moved slowly and added buffalo chips to the miner's stove some buffalo hunter had brought in.

"I'm going to make it," he assured himself. "Doggone if I won't." He lifted his cup of coffee and watched the narrow trail into the clearing. "If those buffalo come up this way, I'll be safe enough until the Comancheros begin to look at all the camps in the canyon, but that'll be a couple of days.

Rance carefully walked into the clearing, stashed his saddle in the dugout and shooed his mare into a rock-walled corral beside the dugout.

Grunting as they moved, the buffalo slowly started up the canyon.

He watched through the opening and grinned, but his grin vanished.

Three horsemen were grouped and waiting, watching the buffalo and studying the canyon.

It's too far to know, he thought, but they don't look like cowboys. I'd better figure they're Comancheros. He looked at the dugout chimney, afraid the smoke would show. The breeze was dispersing it.

"I'd better get ready if they check this dugout." He turned and studied the clearing. "The dugout looks empty but there's tracks that I'd better brush out." He found a broken mesquite branch and began brushing away the hoofmarks of his buckskin. He worked slowly, paused and rested. "Dammit, but I'm tired," he growled. "I've got to get some rest."

The three riders wheeled their horses and cantered them up the canyon.

Rance watched from the opening. "They're Comancheros!" He moved to the side, back of a boulder, and checked the loads in his carbine.

If they see this clearing and check it, he reminded himself, I can't let any of them get away, or I'll have a hundred men to fight. He sighed, rechecked the loads in his carbine and relaxed against a sun-warmed boulder until he heard the horses.

They rode into the clearing, three riders, Comancheros who were swarthy and mean, carrying carbines butted against their legs. They rode their horses slow, and the gunbelts that hung from their shoulders slashed across their bodies.

Rance felt the stabbing pain of his wound, but he ignored it as he cautiously watched the three riders.

The lead horseman saw the buckskin, swiveled in his saddle and discovered Rance.

As his eyes widened, Rance pointed his carbine and settled the front sight on his target.

The third rider's carbine was leveled. He fired.

The ricochet showered Rance with rock chips. His carbine recoiled as he began firing at the three men.

45

The first rider doubled over and slid slowly out of his saddle.

The third man's carbine twisted crazily and fired into the air. His horse reared suddenly, wheeled, and the Comanchero weaved as he clung to the horn of his saddle. His hand slipped, he rolled out of his saddle and sprawled on the ground.

The second man spurred his horse to escape.

Rance levered and fired.

His bullet caught the rider plumb center. He rolled out of his saddle, bounced and skidded on the ground.

As suddenly as the fight started, the quiet came.

Gunsmoke drifted in the clearing and Rance slowly came to his feet. He could smell its acrid bite, shook his head and shrugged. "I can get a few hours sleep before anyone else shows up."

Rance's buckskin followed the trail around a boulder and onto the Panhandle. He straightened from a hunkered position in his saddle and looked back at the trail. It lay hidden in the dark shadows of the moon. The wind was cold. It cut through his jacket, and he could feel the damp chill of night.

What would normally be dry lake beds were filled with rainwater that glistened in the moonlight.

An owl fluttered from a scrawny mesquite and disappeared into the false dawn that lighted the eastern sky, and a coyote standing beside a mesquite gave him a startled look, then loped down the trail.

"I sure as hell should leave well enough alone and

46

go visit the Dutchman on Yellow House Creek, but Garvey owes me some horses, and I have a month's pay coming."

Laura Green relaxed on a bench beside the door of her store and watched a broadwinged hawk lazily circle in the rising wind currents. She raised a steaming cup of coffee to her lips and sipped.

If my figuring's right, she thought, Anson'll come courting today. She smiled contentedly. "He's about ready to pop the question." She spoke the words almost happily. "If he don't, I will. I'm getting tired of waiting. He's not much, but it's comforting to have a man around."

Her smile vanished as she heard the sounds of horses and she looked up.

Billy Joe and Bob reined their horses to a stop as they entered the clearing.

Laura shook her head. "Two no-goods and they belong to Anson. It's comforting to know he didn't father them." She stood. "Get off my property!" She called. "You ain't welcome here and you never will be."

"Ma'am," Billy Joe called, "we know you ain't proud of us, but we're looking for a drifter and maybe you can help. We'll be beholding."

Laura stood and settled her hands on her hips. "If I know I'll tell you, but don't get down."

"Yes, ma'am. There's a drifter we met on the trail yesterday and we're trying to find him. Bob's been winged and he ain't much help."

Bob sheepishly grinned and raised his bandaged arm.

Laura wanted to laugh. She shook her head. "You're the first people I've seen today."

"Was there a drifter through here yesterday or the day before?"

Laura paused. I sure hate lying, she thought.

Billy Joe tilted his head and watched her.

She nodded. "A drifter stopped by."

"Would you know where he went?"

"No. Can't say I do for sure, and I wouldn't tell you." She waved her hand abruptly. "Get going or I'll point the way with my carbine."

Bob wheeled his horse, but Billy Joe waited and studied Laura. "Which way did he go?"

"I don't know and I don't care." Her voice dropped and she reached inside the door for her carbine.

Billy Joe wheeled and followed Bob. "She knows more'n she's telling."

"That may be," Bob answered, "but she was reaching for a gun, and I don't want to tangle with her."

Billy Joe laughed uneasily. "She sure was, and maybe she run us off. She's a heller, but if she marries Anson, I won't run. I'll kill her."

"Pa won't like that."

"He ain't our pa," Billy Joe snapped, "and don't you call him pa, kicking maw out like he did."

"He had reason enough, I guess, when he found out she had bedded down with some drifters. What's done is done." Bob shrugged and changed the subject. "I figure we can check as far as the

Matador, then come back by."

Rance cautiously reined his buckskin onto the flat and studied Laura's store.

The clearing was empty of life and only the burro bothered to raise its head.

Laura stepped through the door and waved. "There's no one here," she called. "Come on in."

As he reined the mare to a stop, Laura met him and took the reins.

"I'll take her back to the store." Her voice was quiet, and her eyes watched the Matador Trail.

He moved to the hitching rail and leaned against it.

"You been shot?"

He nodded.

"Get inside pronto." Her voice had a sense of urgency. "And unbutton your shirt."

"Yes, ma'am."

He moved into the saloon and rested against the bar as Laura came through the door. "Billy Joe and Bob Canutt just passed by and they were asking for you."

"I don't know them." He winced and caught his breath as she probed the wound.

"They're a couple of no-goods who're riding with that carpetbagger Bart Ledbetter." She reached over the counter for salve and bandages.

"Their names are familiar. I think I ran into them yesterday when I had a shooting scrap with them at Tafoya's camp." He caught his breath as she splashed the wound with horse liniment.

"Take it easy."

"Garvey was by. He said you stampeded about two hundred and twenty head of good riding stock right through Tafoya's camp like some wild Apache."

He grinned as she laughed. His voice had lost its humor and he sounded tired. "I'm going to have to hole up somewhere until this gunshot heals."

"Garvey said for you to hightail it to his ranch."

"How do I get there?"

"There's a shortcut you can take through the first ravine west of here."

"Is that the one with the rattler den? I could smell them."

She nodded. "There are three dens on the west side. It's safe enough for another few days, then they'll be edgy. They're getting ready to den. On the east side of the ravine, just past a boulder on the left, a trail will take you up the side of the ravine."

"From the ravine, where do I go?"

"Follow the trail." She set a bottle of whiskey on the counter. "Take a jolt of this now and take it with you."

"I don't want you involved in this." He straightened. "I'll scoot over to Garvey's place."

"They don't scare me, but you need to rest a couple of days. I'll get your horse." She turned to the door and stopped.

Billy Joe stood in the doorway. The sun cast his shadow across the floor and it moved like the devil incarnate.

5

"I didn't knock," Billy Joe said bluntly. "I figured it was a waste of time."

Rance thumbed the holster latch from the hammer of his Walker Colt, turned and eased himself away from the bar. "Leave Laura out of this," he said. "I'm the one you want."

Billy Joe laughed. "I ain't gunfighting you. Tafoya wants to see you and we're going to show you the way."

Laura moved around the end of the bar and wiped her hands on the bar towel. "I've got some good whiskey," she said brightly. "Drinks are on the house."

"Maybe later," Billy Joe said. He continued to watch Rance. "Right now, me'n Bob's got something else in mind. Ain't that right, Bob?"

A window of greased deer hide near the door slid to the side, and Bob stood at the window, his sixgun pointed.

Rance glanced at the window when he heard Laura's voice.

"Oh, no you don't!"

He backed away from the bar to keep both men in sight.

Laura brought a double-barreled shotgun over the bar and leveled it at Bob.

Her body held against the recoil as the first barrel's charge ripped at the window. Wood splinters spun in the air, and gunsmoke mushroomed into the room.

Bob ducked away and Rance could hear his curses.

Billy Joe shifted to keep his eyes on Rance.

Laura smoothly swiveled and fired the second barrel as Billy Joe retreated through the door. He reappeared beside the buckshot shattered jamb, as Rance pointed his Walker Colt.

He felt the sixgun recoil as his bullet splintered the jamb beside Billy Joe's head.

Bob reappeared in the window.

Rance thumbed a shot. Misfire. Damm that nipple, he thought and fanned a shot.

Gunsmoke filled the room. The breeze moved it enough for Rance to see Billy Joe in the doorway. He fired and missed. Crouch-walking to the wall, he eased himself toward the door and cautiously watched for a target.

Hidden by the rolls of gunsmoke, Billy Joe slipped into the room.

Rance crouched against the wall and waited for a sight when the smoke cleared.

As Laura called a warning, Bob leaned through the window and clubbed him with his sixgun.

Rance gasped, tried to raise himself as Bob slashed a second time.

Paralysis ran through his body, and he crumpled to the floor, tried to raise himself but sagged back.

Satisfied that Rance was unconscious, Billy Joe moved across the room, grasped the shotgun and threw it against the wall. He leaned over the bar and glared at Laura. "You stay right there or I'll flat kill you now and not wait till you marry Anson." His arm swept away the cups and glasses Laura had placed on the bar. They shattered and rolled on the floor. "He kicked maw out and he ain't going to have another woman."

Laura watched in stony silence.

"Let's get him outside." Bob took the whiskey that Laura had set out for Rance and followed Billy Joe as he dragged Rance into the clearing.

"Where's his horse?" Bob's eyes searched the clearing. "We can get him to Tafoya's camp before dark."

"We've got time." Billy Joe grinned. "Let's have some fun."

"Like what?" Bob raised the whiskey bottle and drank.

"Like horsewhipping."

Bob laughed. "We can tie him to the corral railing and take turns."

Rance's mind began to clear as he felt them tying his hands to the corral railing. He instinctively clutched at Billy Joe's hair with his free hand and pulled.

His yell was sudden. He felt Rance's arm encircle his neck and pull him off balance.

Rance drew Billy Joe to him, wrapped his legs around his body and began to rake with his spurs.

He twisted and gagged from the choking of Rance's arm.

53

Bob moved in and clubbed with his sixgun.

Rance sagged against the corral. Blood matted his hair and ran down the side of his face.

"I'm going to horsewhip him for sure," Billy Joe growled. "Hold his hand and I'll tie it to the railing."

They held his hand and tied.

"Let's get at it. Bob, you start, and when you get tired, I'll take over."

Rance heard the whisper of a doubled rope and felt the jolting pain again and again.

His consciousness faded.

The pain had stopped until he moved his head, then it racked his body.

He raised his head in defiance.

They rested and laughed at Rance.

He could see Laura in the doorway cradling her head on the shattered jamb. She was crying.

Billy Joe rubbed his jaw. "Tafoya didn't say anything about the drifter's condition."

"He ain't in the best shape now."

"We can do better." He laughed. "Let's get his pants down and see if we can castrate him by shooting at him from here."

"Not me!" Bob shook his head in disbelief. "I wouldn't do that to any man."

"Sure you would." Billy Joe's face hardened. "Brother Bob, you'd like that." He slipped his sixgun from its holster. The sound of a cocking hammer was loud.

Bob shook his head and looked away. "You don't want to do that, Billy Joe."

His laugh was harsh. He fired at the ground at

Bob's feet. The bullet richocheted away as both men looked at each other.

Bob warily watched his brother's eyes squint evilly. "I'm not gunfighting you."

"That's right. You're going to help me teach this drifter a lesson."

Bob paused and studied his brother. He sighed. "All right. We better spread-eagle his legs."

"And when you shoot," Billy Joe ordered, "you better not kill him just to keep him from acting funny like." He walked to the corral fence.

A bullet ripped at the railing. Splinters spun in the air as it ricocheted away.

Billy Joe turned on his heels.

A second bullet plowed the earth at his feet.

Laura Green stood in the doorway of her store levering a cartridge into her carbine.

He ran to the side and back of Laura's store.

Bob crouched and began firing at Laura.

She eased herself into the shadows of the store and fired at Bob.

Billy Joe crouch-walked along the side of the store and paused at the doorway. He listened and suddenly lunged into the room.

Bob watched as Billy Joe began firing.

As suddenly as the shooting started, it stopped and Billy Joe stepped from the store.

"Dead?"

He nodded, turned and looked back at Laura's store. "Let's finish with the drifter and take him to Tafoya."

Rance had raised his head. He knew that Laura was dead, and his tears made trails of anger on his

55

blood-smeared face.

Billy Joe swaggered toward Rance. "That bitch won't be giving us any more trouble." He laughed. "She can wait in hell for Anson."

Blood pounded in Rance's ears. He lunged at Billy Joe. The corral railing held him and he struggled to free himself.

Billy Joe began to laugh. He heard a voice and twisted his body.

Rance turned and watched a squat dumpy man with a face that was flint hard moving across the clearing. The Henry rifle in his hand seemed to be a part of the old man, and he walked with a lurch because of a broken leg that had set bad.

"Bob, Billy Joe, what the hell are you doing?"

Bob turned away.

"What's it to you?" Billy Joe's jaw jutted at the old man and he spit.

"Answer my question," he ordered. "I'm still your pa and I'll whale you to an inch of your life. I can still do it, and don't you forget it."

Billy Joe suddenly grinned. "We rode up to the store and found this drifter just after he'd killed Laura."

The old man stopped, looked toward the store and broke into a run. "Laura!"

Billy Joe watched the old man pause in the doorway and enter. He turned to Rance and grinned. "I figured on killing you." He hitched up his gunbelt. "But we'll let Anson do it for us." His grin turned into a laugh.

"Here he comes," Bob warned.

Anson stepped through the doorway and walked

slowly to them. Tears glistened on his cheeks. He stopped beside Rance. "Did you kill her?"

Rance shook his head. "Billy Joe did."

Billy Joe laughed uneasily.

"Did you kill her, boy?" He turned to his son.

"Hell no!"

"Look at his gun and look at mine," Rance suggested. "He didn't just ride in here. We were shooting at each other."

"You lie about one thing, you'll lie about another." Anson levered a cartridge into his rifle. "And I don't have to look close to see them busted caps." He moved around to keep his back away from Bob.

"All right," Billy Joe snapped. He settled his body and watched Anson. "I killed her. Sure as hell did. Three bullets right into her gut, and she died hard. Like I told you," he glared at Anson, "you ain't going to have any woman as long as I live."

Anson paled.

Rance's fury swelled into a roar and he lunged at Billy Joe.

The railing groaned, slipped and gave way.

He felt the railing loosen. His boots churned into a lunge that carried him toward the two brothers.

Bob turned, drew and fired. His bullet ricocheted from the railing.

Billy Joe gave a startled look as Rance twisted and swung the railing like a club. The railing end crashed into Billy Joe's face. He reeled back, tripped and fell.

Rance's lunge carried him past Billy Joe and toward Bob. He stumbled and fell.

Bob ran to his horse.

Billy Joe rolled to his feet and ran.

Anson began to curse Billy Joe as he fired at him. His bullets threw up puffs of dust and ricocheted as they followed the running man.

Lunging for his horse, Billy Joe tripped. He cartwheeled and slid underneath his horse. It jumped and kicked but missed the scrambling man. He came to his feet cursing and swung into the saddle.

Bob wheeled his horse and spurred it into a gallop ahead of his brother.

Anson lowered his rifle as the two brothers disappeared, and he looked curiously at Rance, who had twisted himself into a sitting position.

He was patiently worrying his hands free of the rope. "Can you help me?"

Anson wiped his eyes and plunged his hand into a pocket for a Barlow knife. "I'll get the rope," he said and lowered his rifle to the ground.

The two men squatted against Laura's storefront. Rance had gotten coffee from Laura's coffee pot, and they silently drank the coffee and watched a broadwinged hawk soar on the rising wind currents.

"You say your name's Long Roper?" Anson looked at Rance.

He nodded.

"I've got some burying to do. You can get on your way." His words were blunt.

"I figured to bury her."

"You're a drifter and I got no use for drifters. I'd take it kindly if you'd go."

Rance could feel the antagonism of Anson, and he resented the old man's attitude. "I'll go when it's done and not before."

"I said git!"

"Mister, I came down off the Panhandle heading for Dallas. I've been chased, beat up, horsewhipped, shot at and hit. Laura's the only person in this whole goddamn Caprock country who treated me like people. She saved my life." He pushed himself to his feet and turned to face Anson. "Not you or any other damm shanty rancher is going to keep me from burying Laura proper like. Then I'm going hunting."

Anson looked up at Rance. He nodded, and his face drew itself tight as he began to cry. "We'll bury her up on the hill in back." He stood. "I'll appreciate it if you'll leave me with her for a while."

6

The trail was four wagons wide and overgrown except for a winding path that led them through a jumble of mesquite and cedar. It wound haphazardly around boulders and rocky dry washes of sand and gravel.

Rance was satisfied to let Anson lead. He was tired, sore and felt as woebegone as a hound dog that had been bested by a skunk.

Anson turned in his saddle and looked at Rance. "It ain't much more to go. After we get over this ridge, it's about a mile along the ravine to where it opens out onto a flat. My shanty's across the flat."

Rance nodded and stretched his back muscles. The pain isn't as bad as it was, he thought. He called to Anson. "Those two boys of yours, where do you think they've gone?"

"Not far." He gestured to the west. "They're probably watching the ranch from a camp they've got up on the rimrock."

Rance could see the rimrock from the trail, and he studied it. "Do you think they know I'm with you?"

"I don't think so. No need to worry. I'm going to stash you out in a dry camp till dark when it's safe to settle you in the house."

"I'm not worrying much. I just like to know where everybody stands." He half smiled. "I sure don't like imposing."

"It's no bother, and I like having someone to talk with."

Rance dismounted in the dark, and he waited while the old man took their horses to a corral and shed in the back. The shanty was a rickety two-room house that had seen better days.

"I'll keep your buckskin in the shed, where she's out of sight," he said as he led their horses to the corral.

Anson returned from the corral and led Rance into the shanty. "It ain't much," he said and gestured to a table and chairs. "It's comfortable since Sarah left."

"Left?" Rance looked sharply at Anson. "I figured she might have died."

"No, she didn't die." He sighed. "Fact is, she's probably whoring over in Fort Worth."

"You don't have to tell me." Rance felt uncomfortable as Anson continued.

"It ain't no secret, so you might as well know. I found out soon after we moved up here from Fort Worth that she likes men. Fact is, she was proud of it, and if you wore pants, it wasn't safe to show up on this flat."

"I'm sure sorry to hear that."

He nodded. "I didn't say much till after the boys came. Then, after a few years she started throwing it up to me, that I wasn't worth going to bed with. That was too much because there ain't a woman I haven't satisfied. I didn't appreciate it, so I kicked her out. That was when she told me that the boys were whelped by a couple of drifters. Damn her soul."

"And they stayed with you?"

He nodded. "She didn't want them."

"It's easy to understand their turning wild, but mean's a different thing." Rance rubbed his neck and watched Anson from the corner of his eye. "It's only fair to tell you that I aim to kill Billy Joe for what he done to Laura." He cautiously watched Anson.

He evaded Rance's eyes and studied his hands. He shook his head. "They deserve it, lordie they do, but I just can't force myself to think about it." He looked at his hands and shrugged. "If you do kill him, I'll probably kill you. They're all the kin I got."

"I figured you should know."

"Laura was a good woman, and I guess I loved her. She's gone and no use crying over spilled milk," he said simply and stood up from the table. "How about beans and biscuits for supper?"

The sounds of a horse slowing from a canter and someone knocking on the door brought Rance out of a sound sleep. He heard the floor creak as Anson crossed the other room and opened the door. Their words were low and he couldn't hear. He cautiously probed under the pillow for his sixgun. Anson's boys are out there somewhere, he thought. If they bust in here, they'll have me by the short hairs.

The door closed and Anson moved around the room as the rider cantered his horse away.

Rance had buckled his gunbelt and settled it on his hip when Anson entered the room.

"How do you feel?"

"All bushy tailed and ready to go. Except for the bullet hole, I feel good and as ready to ride as ever, if that's what you mean."

"Fact is, I do mean that. That was one of Garvey's riders." Anson scratched his jaw and continued. "He said that Childress and the Matador foreman will be at Garvey's place tomorrow to get their horses. He figured you should be there to collect your cut."

"How far?"

"You'd have to start by noon to make it before dark. It ain't far but the trail's up and down."

"Is there a back way I can use? I don't like the idea of getting bushwhacked."

"My boys?"

He nodded.

"I took a ride last night and checked their camp. They've been gone a couple of days."

As Bart Ledbetter watched, High Pockets shifted from his bootheel squat and leaned forward to feed the campfire. It popped and flamed up as he rearranged the wood. He glanced to the side at Joe Lemmon and Asa Range.

Asa and Joe sourly studied the fire. Joe fingered his pocket for tobacco and rolled a cigarette.

Bart watched High Pockets rock back on his boot-heels.

"Something in your craw?" Bart asked.

High Pockets shifted the tobacco in his jaw and spit at the fire. He looked sidewise at Ledbetter and nodded. "You've got a fair bunch of riders who do pretty much what you say." He gestured at the men resting around the fire. "I can't talk for them, but something's bothering me."

"Then get it out." Ledbetter shifted his body and stood as he watched High Pockets.

"Well, I had an uncle that I was real partial to. I was four or five when he went to the Alamo and he didn't come back. Santa Anna and his Mexicans killed my uncle along with Jim Bowie and Davey Crocket. It sure upset me some."

"That's done and forgotten."

"Not by me," the tall man growled. His eyes narrowed. "Pa was with Sam Houston when they caught Santa Anna at San Jacinto and beat the pants off him and his Mexicans. Pa caught a bullet in his leg and came up lame, and I had to do most of the work around the place."

"What the hell are you trying to say?"

"I don't like Mexicans. Asa and Joe too. We don't aim to ride with them."

"There's a lot of money to be had."

"I'll live on mealy beans and sow belly before I'll ride with them Comancheros."

"Anyone else feel that way?" Bart looked at his men. "If you don't like it here, you don't have to stay. I ain't your keeper."

"I feel like High Pockets does." Asa Range stood.

"And me." Joe Lemmon threw his cigarette away and rose to stand beside High Pockets and Asa.

"Then get your horses and ride."

The three men turned from the fire.

As Ledbetter cautiously watched, the tall man turned back. "And I've got a debt to pay." His hand dropped and came up with a sixgun. Bart saw the reflection of the fire on metal and moved his hand in a cross draw, twisted to the side and settled into a crouch.

Asa turned with High Pockets. His sixgun began to clear as the tall man pointed and fired.

Bart's Colt cleared, pointed as his left hand fanned. He heard a bullet ricochet as his gun recoiled.

High Pockets's body twisted and Bart could see the billowing of his shirt as the blood and muscle erupted between High Pockets's shoulder blades.

Ledbetter smoothly swiveled and fired at Asa.

The firelight that reflected in Asa's eye vanished as the back of his head exploded blood and brains into the air.

Joe began to run. He stumbled as Bart's bullet caught him in the back. His head came up, he fell forward and slid into a twisted heap.

Bart walked to High Pockets's crumpled body and squatted on his heels. "You couldn't leave well enough alone. You had to try." He pointed his Colt and fired.

The crumpled man's arm jerked, his leg doubled and slowly relaxed.

High Pockets's gun lay on the ground and Bart grasped it. He turned to face the sprawled Joe

Lemmon and smoothly cocked, pointed and fired at Joe.

His body jerked with the bullet's impact.

Bart stepped to each man, took his money belt, gun and gunbelt. He stood and turned to the men around the fire. "Get them out of here."

Bart patiently inspected his reloaded Colt and nodded. He carefully fitted caps on the nipples and settled the sixgun into its holster.

A tall stringbean of a man hurried into the clearing from a game trail and waved. "Riders!" He gestured to the west. "Twenty or thirty."

Bart came to his feet as a rider walked his horse into the clearing. He was a Comanchero, cautiously studying the clearing and probing with his carbine for a target. His horse gingerly moved to the side as a second and third rider eased into the clearing.

Bart watched the Comancheros move around the clearing and he waited.

They sat their horses, carbines carefully searching for a target.

Tafoya walked his horse into the clearing and reined to a stop. "Senor Ledbetter." He nodded to Bart and dismounted. "We heard shooting." He looked at the three bodies that had been dragged to the side.

Bart laughed. "Three of my men didn't like the way things were going."

"My Comancheros?"

He nodded.

"They did not like riding with Mexicans?"

"Some people carry hates."

"And all of you shot them?"

Bart shook his head. "I do my own killings."

66

Tafoya smiled quietly. "Yes. You would do that."

"Sit." Bart gestured to the fire. "The best I can offer is whiskey or coffee."

"Whiskey," Tafoya grunted as he settled on his bootheels. He twisted his body, took a porcelain cup from one of his men and carefully inspected it. "You have plans to raid the ranchers?" He swung his hand to the north. "Senor Childress and the other gringos?"

Ledbetter nodded and poured whiskey for Tafoya. "The last couple of winters have been mild and most of the colts came through fine. So nearly all of the ranchers have a good supply of horses."

"Cattle?"

"Them too."

Tafoya nodded. He looked up quickly. "The Matador?"

"No. It's spread out over a lot of acres. Their cattle and horses are scattered in a hundred or more canyons and ravines. It'd be tough to catch them up. You'd have to use narrow, winding trails to move them to the Panhandle."

"Perhaps. But I've traded with Indians for horses· and cattle that came from the Matador."

"They could do it with a few head."

"I think," Tafoya said quietly, "perhaps you are afraid."

"And I think," Bart growled, "without your men, I'd kill you."

"I'll consider your thoughts." Tafoya stood and handed the cup to his man. "Perhaps we can still ride together." He rolled a cigarette and lighted it.

"Have another drink," Bart urged.

Tafoya studied him, smiled and motioned for his cup. He glanced at the bodies of the three men and spit. "They didn't like my people," he said sourly and raised his eyes to Bart. "I don't like gringos." The threat of his words hung in the air. He smiled quickly. "But I like money more."

Bart relaxed and smiled. "I could be a friend of the devil if there was money to be had."

Tafoya laughed. "Bueno. We will be amigos."

"What about a raid on Childress?"

"Si, and the Matador, and Senor Garvey." He gestured with his hand. "All of your Caprock country."

Bart nodded and waited.

"My Comancheros are riding," he said proudly. "They will learn the trails to all the ranches."

Ledbetter shifted uncomfortably and his face grew solemn. "No need for that. We'll show you the trails. I figure that's the way to do it."

"No, senor. We will know the trails. Then we will ride as friends not servants."

"Comancheros on the trails will make the ranchers afraid. They know of your Comancheros."

"And they will know of them more." Tafoya's smile was evil. "I have found," he continued, "the ranchers can not depend on help from their government." He laughed abruptly. "This is a good time to take what we want." His teeth gleamed with a sardonic smile. "A good time."

Rance reined his buckskin to a stop in the long slanting shadow of a boulder. He fingered a sack of

Bull Durham and papers from his shirt pocket, troughed the paper and filled it for a cigarette. As he rolled the cigarette and pinched its end, he studied the Garvey Ranch.

Across the open flat, a jumble of corrals crowded against a squat stone ranch house and buildings. Two horses idly switched their tails and waited at the hitching rail for their riders. A thin column of smoke drifting up from a chimney and a fireplace flue added to a thin blue cloud of smoke that drifted across the flat.

Rance winced with the jab of pain from his gunshot as he twisted suddenly. The voice he heard was quiet and blunt.

"Don't move!"

Slowly raising his hands, Rance shifted his body.

"Slow and easy, mister."

A young woman, too old to be silly and too young to be old, sat on a blaze-faced dun and held a carbine pointed at him. "Who are you and what are you doing on Garvey land?"

Rance swallowed. His mouth felt dry. "Ma'am, I'm Rance Long Roper, and please take it easy on that trigger." He tried to smile but it was a washed-out grin.

"I can handle a rifle."

"I sure hope so."

"Dad said you were riding a buckskin with stocking rear feet and that's what you're straddled on." She smiled and eased the carbine off cock. "We thought you'd be riding the other trail."

"The other trail's sure got to be better than this one. I've never seen such a trail before. More boulders and rocks, prickly pear and cactus grass than any one trail deserves. It's sure puny for traveling."

She laughed. Light and lilting like a mocking bird, he thought. "Why did you use this trail?" she asked.

"Some mustangers I saw a few days ago took a dislike to me. One of them by the name of Billy Joe tried to kill me, and he did kill Laura Green."

"Laura?" Her face paled. "Oh, my God!"

"Yes, ma'am. I feel the same way."

Tears glistened on her cheeks as she wheeled her horse and spurred it into a hard run across the flat.

He watched the girl as she disappeared in the distance. "Miss Laura will be missed for sure." He spurred his buckskin into a slow canter toward Garvey's ranch house.

7

One of the three saddled horses at the hitching rail had been ridden by the girl he had met. They raised their heads, watched Rance rein to a stop and dismount, then lowered them to wait for their riders.

As he walked to the door it was opened by Garvey. "Rance Long Roper, come in." He motioned Rance into the room and closed the door behind him. "You met my daughter," he said and nodded to a girl in jeans, a flannel shirt and loosely falling hair that hung to her shoulders. She sat on an overstuffed chair in the corner, and the tears on her cheeks were still wet.

She nodded her head and looked away.

"Yes, sir, I did."

"Did you tell her right, that Billy Joe killed Laura?"

"I saw it, and he did."

"That damm Billy Joe is no good, killing Laura. There's not a person in the Caprock country who doesn't love her, and someone's going to kill him for it."

"I aim to." Rance's words were emotionless and final.

"You've only known her for a couple of days. Why you?"

"She treated me like folks and, for a drifter like me, that doesn't happen very often. She saved my life and was killed for it." He paused, glanced down, then raised his head. "She was a good woman, and her kind is hard to find. She deserves someone to stand up for her."

"There are a lot of men who think your way." He walked to the kitchen and returned with a cup of coffee. "This coffee is strong. It should taste good." He handed the cup to Rance and relaxed in a chair.

"It sure will." Rance took the cup and cradled it in his hand as the girl stood.

"I'll get you a cup, Dad."

Garvey nodded. "Since you've met my daughter, I'll introduce you to her."

Rance grinned.

"This is Sue Garvey." He nodded as she handed him a cup of coffee.

She smiled and her eyes held Rance's for a moment, then she turned away.

"She should be married and raising a cavvy of colts," he continued, "but she figures to stay around the ranch and play hard to get."

"Dad, don't say things like that." She whirled away and angrily walked into the kitchen.

Garvey laughed and looked fondly at his daughter as she watched from the kitchen.

Rance shifted his feet and looked at his cup of coffee. He didn't know what to say.

Garvey turned and Rance looked up as they heard voices in the yard and a heavy pounding on the door.

Garvey smiled and nodded.

"That sounds like Childress." He walked across the room. "He's not backward about knocking."

Sunlight streamed through the door and threw the shadow of a tall compact man diagonally across the floor.

"Garvey, howdy." His strong voice carried a note of friendliness.

"Childress, you're looking good." He took Childress's hand and drew him into the room. "Long Roper's here, come on into the house."

Childress looked at Rance as he walked into the room.

A short slender man standing behind Childress smiled as Garvey took his hand. He followed Childress into the room, nodded to Sue, and stood beside the rancher.

"Jess Crowder," Garvey grunted. "You're as stringy and short cut as ever. I thought the Matador would give you a chance to fill out."

Jess shook his head. "They don't pay you to lazy around and get fat."

Rance stood as Childress walked into the room. Unsure of what would happen, he felt the probing eyes of the rancher, wiped the palm of his hand on the seat of his pants and waited for Childress's hand.

"You're the man we came to see." The rancher continued to study Rance.

He nodded and waited.

"By God, you put a crimp in Tafoya's tail." He grinned and reached for Rance's hand.

He smiled.

Childress turned to Garvey. "There's so damn many rustlers and mustangers that's been hitting me," he growled, "I get a short count every time I do a roundup." He turned back to Rance. "Someday my craw's going to get full, and I'm going to New Mexico and claim every horse and cow carrying my brand. If I could get two more people like you, I'd do it tomorrow." He settled himself in a chair and glowered at the floor.

Rance's smile drew down as he sensed a frustration in the rancher's voice. He was dead serious, Rance knew.

"Here's a man you haven't met," Garvey interrupted. He drew Jess Crowder toward Rance. "This is Jess Crowder, foreman of the Matador."

Rance's face brightened. "Hello, Jess."

Crowder grinned. "I wondered if you'd remember."

"I sure do." Rance turned to Garvey. "I met Jess in an alley in Dodge City. We hid out there when a bunch of Texas cowboys were hellroaring one night. Was that last summer or before?" He looked at Jess.

"Last summer."

"Then maybe Jess'll take kindly to giving you a fifth of the horses you recovered for the Matador."

The grin on Jess's face vanished. "Damm me if you want, but I can't."

"Ain't you running the Matador?" Childress turned to Jess. His words were flat and probing.

"Not that you'd know. We're supposed to have a manager, but he spends most of the time in Dallas."

"By damm, Rance's due a fifth. I'm cutting him a

74

share and so should you."

"He's getting a fifth of mine," Garvey added.

"I figure the Matador's big enough to pay their way." Childress glared at Jess.

"If it was me," Jess argued, "I'd do it and more, but I'd be out riding a grub line if I did that. They'll figure that Rance went into Tafoya's camp for Mr. Garvey's horses and the Matador stock just happened to be there. They don't understand how things are done."

"By damm, someone should tell them," Childress growled.

"Don't beat a dead horse," Rance said brightly. "What's done is done. Jess can't change the way they think, besides I don't have a place for them now."

"That's for sure," Jess said with a sigh.

"The way Tafoya's been acting," Childress observed, "they may learn a lot of things."

Garvey looked up. "How's that?"

"My cowboys have been keeping an eye on him, and it don't look good." Childress shifted his body and took a fresh up of coffee from Sue. "He's been in Tule Canyon longer than he should, and there's bands of Comancheros out riding the trails like they're maybe learning where the trails go."

"We've seen the same thing. Strangers in small bands as far south as Yellow House," Garvey added. "Probably over your way too." He turned to Jess.

The Matador foreman nodded. "It don't look good."

"No, it don't," Childress agreed. "I'm stocking up

on ammunition and some carbines, and you better do the same. I don't like the way things are going."

"Too bad we can't get some help up here."

"Tafoya'd chew them up and spit them out." Childress shook his head. "It's best to get your own justice, like it's been as long as I can remember."

"Seems to me," Rance said, "Tafoya's going to need some help."

"He has over a hundred men."

"He doesn't know the country." Rance scratched his head. "He'll need someone to show him the way."

"He's got the carpetbagger," Childress said. "Ledbetter and his bunch are riding with him. At least it looks that way."

"There's a couple of men by the names of Billy Joe and his brother Bob who are supposed to be riding with Ledbetter. Where can I find them?"

Childress looked sourly at Rance. "Poor white trash, that's what they are."

"Where can I find them?"

"Why?"

"To kill Billy Joe."

The rancher's eyes widened. "Why waste the bullet?"

"He killed Laura Green."

Childress paused, leaned forward and studied Rance.

Jess slowly raised his eyes.

"Laura?" Childress shook his head. "You're joking."

"No. I saw him kill her."

"No woman'll be safe." Garvey voiced the fear of

every man in the Caprock country.

"Damn!" Childress stood. "She was a hard woman to do business with, prices sky high but she didn't deserve that." He walked across the room and turned back. His body had tensed. "Are you going after him?"

Rance nodded.

"You get him!" His words were hard and cold. "Damm it, you get him."

Garvey and Sue filled the coffee cups. "If we had some kind of law around here, he could be tried proper," Garvey said. Frustration tinged his voice.

"There ain't none west of Fort Worth or north of Abilene and it ain't much." Childress turned to Garvey. "You make your own justice, and it's got to be hard or it won't work."

"Where can I find Billy Joe?" Rance looked at Childress.

"Ledbetter has a camp west of my ranch. It's in a clearing on the Pease River about halfway to Tule Canyon. Billy Joe is usually there."

"How do I get there?"

"Where the trail from Fort Worth to Adobe Walls parallels the river, there's a big thicket of bois d'arc, and in the middle of it a trail will cut north. It'll lead you to his camp, but you be careful. There have been some Comancheros riding into his camp. They may be camped there."

"They could cause trouble?"

"They sure as hell could. You'll need all the help you can get." Childress turned to the door. "I'll be right back."

The rancher returned with a sixgun in his hand.

"Look at this."

Rance took the gun and slowly turned it in his hands. "Doggone." He looked at Childress. "It looks different, but the balance is good. Is this that Smith and Wesson that shoots forty-fours the same as my carbine?"

"That's it."

"How do you load it?"

"That latch on top of the frame near the hammer, lift it."

He lifted the latch, broke the gun open and grinned. "All at once." He laughed. "You can unload and load all at once. You don't worry about measuring powder and packing each chamber." His eyes crinkled into laugh lines. "I could sure surprise a lot of people with this."

"Do you like it?"

"I sure do. Where can I get one?"

"It's yours. I got this for a friend of mine, but you'll need it more than him."

"I don't know." Rance shook his head. "I don't take handouts. I'll pay you for it."

"It's not a handout. One man can get into Ledbetter's camp without much trouble." He paused and his eyes saddened. "The trail narrows to one horse and twists. More'n one man can't make it or I'd give you every man on the ranch. This is the best help I can give you."

"I'll pay you for it."

"Damm it, Long Roper, Laura was a good friend to me," he growled. "I want to know that I helped get her the justice she deserves." He turned away and walked to the door. "You better practice with that before you head out," he said gruffly. "Just you get him."

Garvey walked to the door and followed Childress out.

Rance looked at Sue. She sat in the corner chair and was crying.

Jess stood. "I'd better be getting. I'm sorry I can't give you the cut of horses. You deserve it."

"Forget it." Rance stood. "I'm going outside and practice."

Garvey stood on the porch and turned as Rance joined him. "Childress went to Laura's to pay his respects. He'll be back before long."

Rance nodded. "Where can I go to practice with this gun?"

Sue Garvey walked toward the sounds of gunfire. Slow paced shots that were evenly spaced and rapid fire rolled their sounds across the flat and echoed from Garvey's stone ranch house.

Rance worked steadily, learning the gun and how it would fan. His draw was smooth, easy and fast.

He stood relaxed and casual, and he studied the knot of a gnarled cedar. Moving his hand back, thumb extended, Rance felt his thumb catch the hammer spur. His fingers locked around the handle of the Smith and Wesson, and he brought the sixgun forward. The holster held the sixgun until it rotated, thumb cocking the hammer. Slipping from its holster, the gun flipped toward its target.

As the knot shattered, Rance felt the recoil, grinned and nodded. Good, real good, he thought.

Sue waited until she saw him looking proudly at the sixgun. "Rance." Her voice was warm and alive.

He turned and smiled sheepishly. "Miss Garvey, I didn't know you were there."

"I came out to see how you were doing."

"Real good, ma'am." He holstered the .44 and tilted his head to study Sue. The dress she was wearing drew tight around her waist, flared into pleats at her hips and down to below her knees.

She raised a hand to her hair as a breeze swirled its loose strands. "Dad wants me to ask if you'd stay for supper." Her lips wanted to smile and laugh lines creased her face.

He nodded absentmindedly as he watched her eyes. His throat was dry and he swallowed. Her eyes, he thought, were so round and clear. "Yes, ma'am," he heard himself say. "I'd be pleased to."

She turned to go but hesitated. "I want you to know, we're happy that you are here."

"Thank you," he mumbled and watched as she returned to the ranch house. Her dress swayed with her walk. She glanced over her shoulder and waved.

"Doggone."

8

Rance could feel the morning chill bite through his jacket as he settled the saddle on his buckskin. She snorted as he cinched it down. Her breath frosted in the air, and she shook the chill from her body.

"Good girl." He patted her neck and drew the cinch tighter. "You get all your friskiness out before I crawl on. I don't want you trying to throw me."

She snorted.

"Rance! Rance Long Roper!" Garvey called to him from the ranch house. "Hold up a minute."

He turned and watched Garvey stumble the morning stiffness from his legs.

He legged himself between the corral railings and walked to Rance. "There's something I want to talk about."

"Is something troubling you?" Rance watched him curiously. He fished the makings from his pocket, rolled a cigarette and waited for Garvey to speak.

"In a way." Garvey slipped his hands into his hip pockets and settled himself. "The damnedest things happen." He scratched his jaw. "I can't figure women, not even when Sue's mother was alive." He pulled at his ear and looked sidewise at Rance. "Sue

81

has never had the time of day for any man she ever met, but you rode in yesterday and she put a dress on. Not only that but she fixed the best damn supper I ever tasted, and she's moony as a mourning dove in the spring.''

"It sure was a good supper.'' Rance felt uncomfortable and he glanced away.

"Did you two sneak out after we went to bed?'' Garvey studied him suspiciously.

"No, sir!'' Rance shook his head.

"Do you have any idea about my daughter?''

"No, sir,'' Rance answered. "She's sure pretty and I'd be proud to call on her.''

Garvey relaxed and grinned.

"Well, you better give it some deep thought, 'cause she's really getting moon eyes. She's got a mind of her own, and if you come calling, it won't set well with her or me if you up and skedaddle.''

"I wouldn't do that,'' he assured Garvey. "I'll give it a lot of thought.''

"That's all I can ask.'' Garvey twisted around to look at the ranch house. He turned back. "Childress and Jess Crowder will be cutting their horses out when their men get here. Childress will leave your share with me, and you can get them when this business is done with.''

"I appreciate that.'' He lifted and settled his gunbelt. "I'm going up towards Ledbetter's camp.''

"You keep an eye on them trails and scoot out if things don't look right.''

Rance reined his buckskin to a walk and looked

back at the ranch. Smoke from the chimney drifted slowly in the morning air, and he wondered if the figure beside the house was Sue.

Thin rolls of fog hung in the ravines and gullies where scattered clumps of cedar and mesquite bulked on the hogbacks and ravines. It's hard to see anyone in the fog, he thought. The trail disappears in it, but the sun will burn it away soon. He cautiously walked the buckskin on a trail that would take them to the Fort Worth-Adobe Walls Trail.

It's early for anyone to be riding the trails, he thought, and the Comancheros are probably still bedded down, but you never know when someone will decide to bushwhack. He looked across the fog-ribbed ridges. Mr. Garvey said the Adobe Walls Trail is about a four-hour ride north, but there's some rough country to go through. He nudged the buckskin. "Let's go."

He could feel the sun on his back and luxuriated in its warmth. The trail led into a clearing on a flat-topped ridge. He reined to a stop, rolled a cigarette and studied the trail where it followed the ravine's crest before dropping to a flat below. Shifting his body, Rance stepped out of his saddle. In the high grass, he moved cautiously and watched for rattle-snakes. They don't always rattle, he cautioned himself. The grass swished around his boots as he walked to a boulder. He paused, settled himself on the boulder and watched the ravine. He could see the trail as it followed the dry bed of a run-off stream until it disappeared into a cluster of mesquite and bois d'arc. Beyond the ravine, the openness of a wide flood plain was inviting.

If there are Comancheros on these trails, he thought, and if they got up early, they've had time to get down this way. He could see what appeared to be a trail across the flat and shook his head. I don't like that. About a mile across the flat and no place to hide. A man in that clump of cedar on the side could hit anything on the flat with a long-barreled rifle. I don't like it. Maybe I'll slip around the edge of the clearing where I'll be close to some kind of cover. He stood, stretched and returned to his buckskin. I might as well get across the flat, he decided.

He reined the buckskin to a stop at the edge of the clearing and studied the trail, shook his head and fingered his pocket for tobacco and papers. It doesn't look any better now than then. He lighted the cigarette and studied the wide clearing. I'm going around. He nudged the buckskin into a walk. The scant sign of a trail around the edge of the clearing reassured him that others had been cautious of riding in the open.

He patiently held the mare to a walk and watched the clearing as he reined her into the tree shadows. I've sure got a feeling about that trail, he thought. Maybe I'm wrong. Maybe I'm imagining things, but I'm not going to rush it. Tafoya didn't get to be the biggest trader in the Panhandle by accident, and he's not going to move this far from the Caprock without knowing the country. If I don't run into some of his Comancheros it'll be an accident.

The far edge of the clearing looked different. Rance reined his mare to a stop and studied the edge of the trees. It looks like something moved, he thought.

What had been only shadows became riders. Three riders sat their horses at the edge of the clearing and studied the trail they were following.

It's too far to see, he decided, but they could be some of Tafoya's Comancheros. He held the buckskin in and waited for them to move into the clearing.

The three riders walked their horses onto the trail. They rode single file and the vaquero slouch of their bodies warned him.

"Comancheros!" His body tensed and he could see the extra gunbelts hanging from their shoulders. They'll sure as hell see the signs of my buckskin on the trail. In case they come back, I'd better find a place to fort up. Better here than on the trail where they can sneak in close.

The riders casually crossed the clearing, almost without a care.

He waited in the shadows of a high growing mesquite and nudged the buckskin into a canter when the three Comancheros disappeared from the clearing. Following the faint trail to a cluster of cedar and mesquite that grew around a jumble of boulders, he reined to a stop and studied the sparse cover on the flat.

The cover gets scant on around the clearing to the trail, he thought. Only a few scrawny cedar beyond this point. This is probably as good a fort as I can find. Legging down from his saddle, Rance led the buckskin to a shelter of cedar and mesquite.

He unbooted his carbine, checked the loads in its

magazine and threaded his way between twisted cedar and mesquite trees to a point that would give him comand of the entire clearing. He settled himself in the shelter of a boulder, rolled a cigarette and waited.

The three Comancheros returned. Rance could see them through the trees, and he watched as they milled their horses at the edge of the flat. One rider dismounted to look for signs and began to circle.

They'll see my tracks for sure, he decided, and crushed the cigarette and settled his body. A bead of perspiration slowly began to edge its way down his backbone as he watched the Comanchero on foot motion to the others.

The two riders slowly walked their horses as they followed their partner along the trail Rance had taken. They moved faster as the man on foot began to trot, and they cautiously watched the clearing.

They'll be on top of me soon, he decided. Before they get too close, I'd better warn them off. He jacked a cartridge into the chamber of his carbine, settled the front sight on a mesquite limb and slowly squeezed the trigger.

The limb shattered and, as the bullet richocheted, the men froze and suddenly whirled their horses away. The man on foot ran awkwardly to his horse and, as it broke into a gallop, rolled into his saddle.

Rance watched them slow to a stop out of carbine range. One good thing about running into them, he decided, it'll keep them away from Sue Garvey. My horses too. He grinned happily. Doggone. Garvey said she's getting moon-eyed. His grin vanished as he watched the Comancheros.

The three riders rode to the center of the flat, wheeled their horses and cantered toward Rance. The middle rider slowed his horse. The others spread wide and raced toward Rance. The center rider broke his horse into a run.

Rance felt his tenseness drain away. He relaxed, rolled his shoulders, and as he watched the three Comancheros race toward him, raised the carbine and waited. One of the riders rode straight in his saddle. Almost like a Texasman, he thought. A good target, he smiled grimly.

The three horsemen neared. Only the sounds of their horses' hoofs and the ring of Spanish bits broke the silence.

The man who rides straight will be easy, Rance decided. He pivoted away from him and pointed at a Comanchero riding hard and low over his horse's back. His front sight settled on the rider, and he levered three .44's at him.

A bullet shattered the pommel of his saddle. Splinters of wood and strips of leather spun in the air as the bullet ricocheted. A second bullet sprayed dirt in front of the horse.

Smoke began to swirl and drift through the trees. The rider reined back in panic.

Levering a cartridge into the chamber, Rance hurriedly swiveled, sighted and squeezed as his sight settled on the tall riding Comanchero's crossed gunbelts.

The gunbelts twisted and jerked.

His body doubled and racked back against the cantle. He straightened and fell forward. His hand grasped the horn, held for a moment, then he slipped from his saddle and rolled on the hard-packed earth into a lifeless heap.

Before the man had slipped from his saddle, Rance turned back to the rider who had panicked. He had swung to the ground, firing his sixgun at Rance as he charged.

Rance felt perspiration itch his scalp as he levered a cartridge and fired. His bullet missed.

The man loomed large.

A bullet tugged at his shirt. Another splintered the twisted limb of a cedar as Rance levered the carbine into a rolling sound of rifle fire that echoed across the flat. Gunsmoke clouded around him and he could smell its acrid bite.

The Comanchero stopped his charge, doubled forward and reeled back. A bullet ripped his shoulder. Bone and muscle collapsed as four bullet holes pinned his shirt against his body and erupted from his back.

Rance heard the sounds of horse's hoofs and looked at the third Comanchero.

He had wheeled his horse and spurred it into a hard run that carried him to the center of the flat. He reined his horse along the trail and disappeared into the trees.

Rance slowly stood and studied the two crumpled bodies. "How did I get into this?" he asked himself. "I was just going to Dallas for the winter," he complained. "I was chased and shot, and a good woman was killed saving my life." His jaw hardened and he angrily looked toward Tule Canyon. "Damn you, Billy Joe," he swore, "by all that's holy, I'm going to get you if I have to kill every Comanchero this side of the Caprock." The anger that boiled in his gut carried him to the two still bodies where he took their gunbelts. "I'll need a lot of ammunition if I'm going after Billy Joe and Tafoya. And if I'm going to court Sue Garvey, I've got to run the Comancheros out of this part of the country." He slung the gunbelts over his shoulders.

The buckskin mare looked curiously at Rance as he led her into the open. The two extra gunbelts were crossed over his body like a hard riding Comanchero. As he booted the carbine, she snorted and shook her head.

"We've got some riding to do." Rance rubbed her neck. "I want to catch the other man before he gets to Tafoya, or they might figure that I'm Garvey and raid his ranch." He legged himself into the saddle and nudged his buckskin into a canter.

The trail followed a sandy-bedded run-off stream that meandered along the windings of a long ravine. The Comanchero's sign was splashed across the sandy floor by the hard running hoofmarks of his horse.

He's running, Rance thought, but he can decide to bushwhack me at anytime. Lord knows it'd be easy to do. He rode steadily and studied the ravine. His back muscles drew tight, and a bead of perspiration worked its way down his back. I'd sure like to sit back and wait, but that'd give him a chance to stop running and start thinking.

The buckskin raised her head, ears forward.

Rance slowed and studied the ravine. Hoofmarks continued around a turn in the sandy floor. A crow squawked angrily and flapped its way into the air from the crowded mesquite that lined the ravine floor.

"Easy, girl." He rubbed her neck and lowered himself to the floor of the ravine. "Let's get over to the side, and I'm going to check that turn in the ravine." Unbooting his carbine, Rance catwalked along the streambed.

His buckskin snorted.

He heard the whinney of a horse ahead of him. He paused and studied the tree shadows. A mockingbird's sudden flight along the ravine startled him, and he squatted. A boulder beside his boot shattered as a carbine ripped the shadows. Sand and gravel filled the air. Rance threw himself to the side and the bullets followed. Gunsmoke rolled away from a tree that hugged the ravine floor.

The Comanchero was well hidden, only the muzzle flashes and smoke that drifted in the wind showed where he had waited for Rance.

He rolled beneath limbs of a mesquite that lined the sandy floor, and the barrel of his carbine projected beyond the trees. He reached for the carbine and paused. He may not know where I am, he thought. If I move the carbine, he will.

The buskwhacker saw the carbine and began to fire probing shots around the rifle. Sand bulged into puffs as bullets ricocheted and whined.

Rance worked his way under the mesquite to a small clearing and came to his feet.

The firing had stopped.

Crouch-walking his way along a game trail that led to the dry stream bed, Rance eased the Smith and Wesson from its holster and stepped onto the sandy floor.

He could see the dim outline of a man in the tree shadows. He was searching for Rance.

"Amigo!" His call spun the man around. As his carbine swung to point, Rance's bullet threw him back against a tree limb. He waited for any movement of the Comanchero, then cautiously moved into the trees.

The Comanchero had dropped his carbine, doubled over and collapsed on the ground. He coughed and wiped his blood-flecked lips as Rance crouched over him.

"Amigo." Rance slowly shook his head. "You're going to die, amigo. Morte."

The Comanchero glared at him.

"Comprende English?"

He nodded sullenly.

"Maybe you can tell me something."

The man spit angrily and shook his head.

"You're going to die. You know that."

He nodded.

"Then you won't mind telling me what Tafoya's going to do."

"Gringo pig!" He spit the words.

"You don't mean that. We're amigos." Rance's smile was humorless.

The Comanchero shook his head, and his body racked with a spasm of coughing.

"You want to look nice when you die," he reasoned, "like a grand vaquero."

The man's eyes brightened. He nodded as a faint smile crossed his face.

"You tell me what I want, and you'll look nice."
Rance's voice hardened. "If you don't, I'll rope drag
you down this stream bed until you're dead." He
looked away.

The Comanchero's eyes widened. "Por favor, no!"

"Si, I will."

He shook his head.

"Tell me."

The Comanchero's shoulder sagged, and he
nodded. "Si, I will tell you."

"What's Tafoya going to do?"

"Raid."

"Who?"

"Senor Childress, Senor Garvey, I heard them
talking, and El Matador."

Rance's smile was sour. "Who was he talking to?"

"The gringo."

"Who?"

The Comanchero shrugged, his head sagged and
he died.

Rance slowly stood. He felt dirty. "A dying man
shouldn't be treated like I did to him." He holstered
his gun and slowly returned to his buckskin.

9

"I shouldn't have treated him the way I did." Rance wiped his mouth as if to clean it of a bad taste. "I don't know how else I could find out about Tafoya." He reluctantly turned and looked at his backtrail. Mesquite and bois d'arc blocked his view of the ravine.

The trail followed winding ravines and gullies to where it joined a wide cut through the ridges. Rance reined to a stop and carefully studied a trail that followed the cut. "This must be the trail to Adobe Walls," he decided. "It's been used a lot by horses and cattle."

The buckskin shook her head as he swung to the ground and led her to the shade of a mesquite. Squatting beside the mare, he rolled a cigarette. If that Comanchero was right, he thought, Tafoya'll raid Mr. Childress first. From his ranch they can get up on the Panhandle before anybody'll know what's happened. He swallowed the dryness in his mouth and shook his head. It'd be just as easy for them to raid Mr. Garvey, but they'd have a longer ride to get to his ranch.

The buckskin's head came up. She looked at the

trail, ears pointing.

Rance came to his feet and drew the mare with him. "Someone's coming." He led her into the trees that clumped behind them, into a small clearing where he squatted on his heels for a better view.

The wide trail seemed empty of life. He heard only the faint sound of horses as a mockingbird chattered angrily at a canyon wren as it flirted in the trees. The creak of saddle leather and ring of Spanish bits came louder. A horse snorted. He heard the muffled sounds of voices—a word, a laugh and quiet. Through the trees, he saw them.

Four horsemen rode in a vaquero slouch, quiet but watching and only an occasional word. One of the men glanced at the trail Rance had used. He reined to a stop and gestured to the trail as the others reined up.

Rance slowly raised and stood, slipped his carbine from its boot and squatted. He eased the lever down, checked the loads and closed it without a sound. Uncertainty and a sense of danger hung on his shoulders.

A rider dismounted and, holding his reins, he walked to the trail and studied the sign. Squatting to examine the tracks, he raised his eyes and looked at the hoofmarks that led to the clump of trees where Rance waited. He stood and surveyed the trail.

Perspiration itched Rance's scalp and his back muscles drew tight.

The Comanchero impassively looked at the trees and beyond. He considered what he saw and turned back to his horse.

One of the mounted men jacked a cartridge into the chamber of his carbine. The sound was loud.

"No!" the man on foot ordered. "No bueno." He motioned for the others to ride and stepped into his saddle.

As they disappeared around a bend in the trail, the tension eased, a crow squawked at an owl, and Rance fingered his shirt pocket for tobacco and papers.

"Whew," he sighed. "Four would have been too many." He lighted the cigarette and inhaled deeply. "They're everywhere. Tafoya must be figuring to raid and it'll probably be Mr. Childress." He stood.

The buckskin followed as he threaded his way through the clump of trees and shook herself as he dropped the cigarette and stepped it out.

"We'd better get over to the Childress Ranch."

Rance saw a band of horses as he cantered his buckskin out of a gully. A thin column of smoke drifted in the air from a windbreak where four men had started a fire. A fifth man stood beside the cowboys who had relaxed into a squat. He turned and waved.

"That looks like Childress."

The rancher walked to meet him. "Have you seen anything?"

"Some." Rance dismounted. "I saw four riders on a wide trail south of here."

"About five miles?"

He nodded.

"That's the trail to Adobe Walls."

"I figure they're Comancheros, and I had a set-to with three others on the trail I took coming up this way."

"Shooting?" Childress watched him closely.

Rance nodded. "They're dead, but before he died one told me that Tafoya is planning to raid you, Mr. Garvey, and the Matador."

"They'll hit the small ranchers too."

"Yes, and it's the womenfolk I'm worried about."

Childress nodded. He looked across the Caprock country and sighed. "We've had trouble with the Indians and rustlers. Now it's the Comancheros."

"It'd be a good idea to tell everyone."

"I aim to." He turned to his men. "Joe, you and Bill get over here." As the two cowboys scrambled to their feet, he turned back to Rance. "Joe's good with a gun. You," he turned to Joe, "head out and warn every rancher you can find that Tafoya's going to raid. You may be too late for some." He slapped Joe on the back. "Get going. If you run into trouble, get your ass back here for help."

Bill waited with Joe. "Do you want me to go with him?"

"No. I want you to go to the ranch, break out the guns and cartridges. Give a carbine and box of cartridges to every man on the ranch." He turned back to Rance. "There's a pot of coffee on the fire. Let's have some."

Rance took a cup of coffee and settled to the ground. "I can't help thinking this wouldn't have happened if I'd have kept my nose out of Tafoya's camp."

"You're way wrong." Childress cleared his throat

and spit. "He almost raided last year, but there was a lot of rain and all the draws and ravines were flooding." He scratched his chin. "We don't know if he'll raid, and there's a big difference between thinking and doing. If he does, we'll be ready for him."

"If Tafoya raids, I think he'll need Ledbetter and his men to guide the Comancheros. If I can find Billy Joe and settle with him, the raids might be delayed and it'd give everybody a better chance to get ready."

"That may be so, but you'd best be careful of yourself. If you get into Ledbetter's camp, watch him. He's dirty mean and tricky."

Rance stood and settled his gunbelt. "I will."

The Adobe Walls Trail narrowed. Rance settled back against the cantle, and his buckskin turned her head to look at him. She snorted impatiently. He ignored her and studied the country.

A roll of dust to the north hung low on the horizon. "It's not the kind of a day for a wind," he said to himself. "If that's a band of horses, then Tafoya's made a raid. Damn it," he grumbled, sighed and looked at his buckskin.

He raised his eyes back to the horizon and straightened. A roll of smoke suddenly curled into the air. "Oh hell!" He wheeled and spurred his buckskin into a gallop along the trail to a cutoff he remembered having passed.

Rance slowed as he neared the burning ranch

house. He reined to a stop as the trail took him onto
a flat. There was a stillness in the clearing. Only
sounds of the fire, crackles, occasional creaks and
sighs as a rafter weakened or burned through
interrupted the calls of mourning doves. He shook
his head.

"Damn," he growled. Anger surged through his
body. "It's got to be the Comancheros. No cattle or
horses around. They raided sure as hell." Rance
swiveled in his saddle as he heard a cow bawl.

From a ravine, a cow scrambled onto the flat. A
second and third followed. Three horsemen appeared
behind the cattle. One of the raiders rump-popped
the rear of a cow. A grin spread across his face.
"Eyaa!"

The buckskin shied back as Rance unbooted his
carbine and swung to the ground.

They saw him and reined to a stop. The cows
wandered across the flat and stopped to graze. One
of the riders gestured to the others and motioned for
them to spread out. He turned to face Rance, rested
his hands on the horn of his saddle and smiled.

Rance moved away from the buckskin, levered a
cartridge into the chamber and waited.

The leader of the horsemen waved with his hand.
"Amigo."

"Who are you and what are you doing here?"
Rance watched the three riders and slowly leveled
the carbine. "Crawl off those horses."

Two of the horsemen unbooted their carbines and
jacked cartridges into the chambers of their rifles.
The sounds hung in the air.

Their leader shrugged and looked at the burning

ranch house. "Senor," he said, "we are helping here." He smiled quickly.

"You," Rance gestured with his carbine, "crawl off that horse pronto."

The leader shrugged and shifted his body. As his leg swung over the cantle, his partners began firing. Their horses wheeled nervously.

Rance pointed and fired.

The leader's body sagged against his horse, he grasped for the horn but fell. As he tried to sit, the Comanchero sagged into a heap.

Rance swung the carbine, levered and fired.

Gunsmoke began to layer in the air. It drifted slowly.

The near rider's horse shied nervously. He attempted to lever a cartridge as his horse whirled, lost his seat and caught his boot in its stirrup. His horse jumped as it felt the spur. He fell and was dragged until his boot came free.

The third man spurred his horse into a hard run across the flat as the second rider groggily came to his feet, caught his horse and scrambled into the saddle.

Rance's bullets followed the two riders. He couldn't get a good sight through the rolling smoke of the ranch house and the gunsmoke that began to cloud and drift.

They disappeared across the flat and their hoof-beats died in the distance.

Rance lowered the carbine and began thumbing cartridges into its magazine. Walking to the still-form of the Comanchero, Rance took his gun and gunbelts. The sixgun was rusty and wired together.

He threw it away, walked to the buckskin and legged himself into the saddle.

The flat seemed desolate. The ranch house had almost burned to the ground. Rafters and beams still outlined the house until a rafter burned through, then they collapsed into the burning remains. A poorly built barn sagged at the corner, and a wagon stood near the windmill. The smell of stale manure, the acrid bite of gunsmoke, and a sense of death hung over the flat as Rance walked his buckskin to the smouldering remains of a hard scrabble ranch.

The three cows and the Comanchero's horse quietly grazed on the short grass as Rance passed.

He neared the ranch yard, reined to a stop and as he stepped down from his saddle, the hard metallic sound of a carbine levered closed warned him.

"You make one move and I'll blow you to hell." The voice was low and gruff. "Git your hands up and turn slow."

Rance raised his hands and slowly turned to face the voice. He saw the man's eyes, wide and squinty, shaded by a dilapidated hat.

He was short bodied and angular, and his face was sandpaper rough. "Who're you and what're you doing on my land?"

"I saw the smoke and thought I could help."

"Who could help against a bunch of devils that would burn a man's home and take his cows? And I don't know but what you're one of them."

"No, sir, mister. I killed—" He started to point but stopped when the man's finger tightened on the trigger. "One of them is over there." He gestured with his head.

"He could be making like dead, till you get me."
His face had soured, but his mouth visibly dropped
when he saw the remains of the ranch house.

Rance watched his eyes as tears formed in their
corners. "I sure wouldn't do that," he said. His body
relaxed and he settled on his feet.

"You're a goddamn liar!" The man's voice rose.

Rance moved as smoke belched from the carbine's
muzzle. Throwing himself to the side, he felt a
burning crease of his shoulder as he sprawled on the
ground. He rolled, swung his body around and came
to his knees, the .44 pointing.

The old man had the lever down ready to close
when he saw the Smith and Wesson pointing and
Rance holding his shoulder with his left hand. "Go
on, kill me and my family. We ain't got nothing left
to work for." His eyes squinted and tears coursed
his wrinkled face.

Rance cautiously stood and eased himself to the
old man. He carefully reached for the carbine.

The man's hands were nearly lifeless as Rance
took the carbine from him, and he cried in helpless-
ness.

"I said I wasn't one of them. You just relax, sit
down and listen 'cause I don't want to do any hurt
to you. I want you to help me bandage this arm."
Rance led him to the side of the shed and turned as
he heard the sounds of a running horse.

A rider on a dun horse waved as he broke onto the
flat. "Mr. Carver, are you all right?" he called and
dismounted as his horse slowed to a walk. He
stopped when he recognized Rance.

101

Rance remembered Joe, whom Childress had sent to warn the ranchers. He nodded and held his shoulder.

Joe saw the blood. "Trouble?"

"More'n enough. Comancheros. I got here when they were leaving and there was some shooting."

"The dead man, did he hit you?"

Rance shook his head. "This man. There was a misunderstanding and—"

The mousy voice of a woman interrupted Rance. "It's Joe Williams." Rance turned and saw a small whisp of a woman push the door of a storm cellar aside and crawl out, followed by two young boys.

Joe listened to the story of what had happened as he bandaged Rance's arm.

"I'm sure sorry about your arm," Carver apologized, "but I don't trust nobody anymore. I just don't know what to do."

"All you can do," Rance said as he flexed his arm, "is keep trying. Nothing in this world is free. Something good will come along."

Joe nodded. "I wish I'd have gotten here earlier."

"Wouldn't have done any good." Carver looked sadly at his burned ranch house. "Must have been six or seven of them. Little Jody here saw them first," he said and nodded at his older boy.

"They sure scared me," the boy said.

Joe turned to Rance. "Are you going to settle with Billy Joe? Your arm's been creased."

"It's not too bad."

"When that's settled, why don't you meet me at Laura Green's? I think I can roundup four or five men who'd like a little excitement. We might be able to put a burr under Tafoya's saddle.''

"If I make it, I'll see you there.'' Rance moved his hand to his holster and checked his draw. He winced slightly and walked to his buckskin.

10

Rance reined to a stop and looked back at the ranch.
The fire had burned itself out. Smoke hung like a
cloud over the small group beside the only building
left standing, and the horse and cows continued to
graze on the short grass.

"I don't care what Mr. Childress said," he
complained. "If I hadn't took back Mr. Garvey's
horses, I don't think they'd have burned out Mr.
Carver. I can't change what was done," he decided,
"but I can sure as hell try to stop Tafoya." He shook
his head sadly. "I don't know how, but I won't feel
right if I don't try."

He nudged his buckskin into a canter on the trail
the Comancheros had used. It ran straight with few
turns until dropping into a wide ravine. The stock
they had stolen left the trail chewed and marked by
their hoofs.

As he followed the winding trail, a single rifle shot
ripped the sandy loam with a spray of dust in front
of ihs buckskin.

He wheeled her to the shelter of bois d'arc and
mesquite that lined the trail, swung to the ground
and checked his carbine. It may be a warning, he

thought, and maybe not. He squatted and eased his head around to watch the clump of trees. A mesquite limb beside his head shattered with a shot. He sprawled back and scrambled to a better shelter.

Gunsmoke drifted in the still air, and he watched it snake along the trail. He's sure enough there, he thought, and I'm going to have to get him out the hard way. Game trails wander all over here, but I don't know if I can find one. He came to his feet, booted the carbine and stepped into his saddle. "You're going to have to do some running." He leaned forward and rubbed the mare's neck. "You're a good horse. Take care of yourself."

He drew his sixgun, took a deep breath and dug his spurs into her flanks.

"Eyahaa!"

The buckskin broke from cover in a hard plunging run. Sand, loose earth, and clods of dirt whirled in the air as the mare charged toward the turn.

He hunkered low in his saddle and watched the trees ahead. The flash of metal, a dim form, and Rance pointed the .44. He dropped the hammer and began to fan as his mare leaned into the turn. The sixgun was empty when he flashed past the bushwhacker's hiding place.

His bullets chewed at tree limbs and whipped them into a shower of splinters and bark bits.

Wheeling his mare into a sheltered area, he rump slid her to a stop. He was on the ground and running back to a clump of trees before she came to her feet.

Through the scant cover of a scrub mesquite, Rance studied the trees that edged the trail. "That's the place where he was waiting, but there's no sign

105

of him." He dumped the empty cartridges from his sixgun and reloaded.

The trees moved only as if a breeze had swayed their tops. A man groaned and coughed. The trees shook wildly, a sound of falling, and a saddled horse walked onto the trail, its empty saddle smeared with blood.

Rance turned and walked to his buckskin. He carefully examined the mare and brushed away smears of sand from her rump. "You look all right." He patted her neck.

She snorted and shook her head.

"We won't have to do that again. I don't think they'll have more than one guard on their backtrail," he assured her and stepped into the saddle.

As he nudged his mare into a walk, Rance watched the trail. The dust that had hung in the air earlier had settled, and the sounds of running stock faded in the distance. This trail will probably join the Adobe Walls Trail where I can find Billy Joe, he thought. He shook his head. If I look for Billy Joe, the Comancheros might start raiding some other little rancher or maybe Mr. Childress. Damn me, he sighed, it's hard to figure just what to do.

The Adobe Walls Trail had narrowed through a bois d'arc thicket. It wasn't too winding, but he slowed to dodge their scraggy limbs. "This is worse than chasing cows out of a cactus patch," he grumbled. And as he ducked a limb, Rance saw the trail.

It was open and inviting but narrowed to rider wide when it began to twist and turn. He studied the trail and shook his head sadly. Chewed up by horses ridden in and out of the thicket, the trail was well used. "It'd be a mistake to go in," he cautioned himself. "I think Tafoya has moved down to this clearing. It's closer to the Childress Ranch." He settled back in his saddle and smiled grimly. The cattle and horses had been driven toward Tule Canyon. When he stood in his saddle, Rance could see the top of a roll of dust ahead of him.

"They're taking the stock to Tule," he said sourly. "If I can stampede Tafoya's stock again, it will slow him down." He shook his head. "I'll have to settle with Billy Joe later."

Rance dismounted from his buckskin in the clearing he had used before. Hidden from the trail except for a narrow opening, he felt safe and rolled a cigarette. He squatted beside the opening, relaxed and enjoyed his smoke. I'll scout around and see what they've got here, he decided. Then, I'll know what I can do. He crushed his cigarette and moved onto the trail.

From the top of a house-high boulder, shielded by a clump of cottonwood, Rance watched the camp. He squatted on a ledge and waited.

The Comancheros were grouped around a fire except for a few who were busy in the corrals.

There are only a few of them here, and I don't see Tafoya. Only two tents are set up. Hell, he must have the rest at Ledbetter's camp. Rance glanced over his shoulder.

Two riders were moving along the trail at an easy

walk. They reined to a stop and led their horses into an opening below the boulder.

He tensed. A bead of perspiration inched its way down his spine.

The horsemen laughed and dismounted.

The creak of leather and sounds of reins dallied on a tree limb warned Rance that they planned to stay. "What the hell are they doing here?" He edged himself away from the crevasse he had used to climb to the ledge.

Boots scraped. Spur rowels rang as the men worked their way up the crevasse.

He backed along the ledge until he could move no more. His eyes scanned the boulder and ledge where he crouched, half hidden by a rocky outcropping. His hand slipped the .44 from its holster and he waited.

The two Comancheros stepped out of the crevasse. One of the men relaxed on the ledge and began to roll a cigarette. His partner turned. He saw Rance and his eyes widened.

Rance pointed the .44 and gestured with it.

The Comanchero backed away, tripped over his partner and sprawled into the crevasse. He grasped for a handhold, missed and began to slide down the crevasse. He rolled and fell to the bottom.

The raider's partner turned in surprise, saw Rance and fumbled for his gun.

Rance cocked the .44 and prodded it in the man's face.

His hands came up.

"Get over there." He motioned with the .44 to a level space. "Belly down."

Scrambling away from the crevasse, the Comanchero spread-eagled himself on the ledge. With his knee in the Comanchero's back, Rance took the tiedown thong from the man's holster and tied his hands. Doubling his legs back, Rance tied the thong end to the raider's spurs.

"That should keep you out of trouble." Rance stood. He cautiously walked to the crevasse and looked down at the man who had fallen.

Sprawled into a crumpled heap at the bottom of the crevasse, the Comanchero didn't move.

It wasn't much of a fall. Maybe he's playing possum, he thought and held the .44 ready as he eased himself down the narrow crevasse.

The man's body was wedged between boulders at the bottom. He didn't move, and his hand fell loosely when Rance touched it. Squatting beside the body, he checked for a pulse. Nothing. He stood and looked at the body, shook his head and turned. I won't have to worry about him. I'm going to have enough trouble with Tafoya, he decided, to worry about anything else.

The buckskin raised her head as he slipped into the small clearing. He rubbed her neck and cinched the saddle down. "I can't do anything here. I'll check the other side of their camp."

The mare wanted to run, but Rance held her back as they followed a trail that circled the camp.

As they neared the Yellow House Trail, he reined her to a stop, stood in his saddle to study the trail. Empty of life, it was inviting, but he cautiously waited and watched the camp.

The Comancheros stood, straggled to their horses

and mounted. Four men remained by the fire.

"Where are they going?" He curiously watched them group around a rider and follow him along the trail toward the Childress Ranch.

"Dammit!" He glowered at the riders. "Too damn many to fight." He shook his head. "If I could get them to turn back to the camp, I'd have a chance to get away and warn Childress."

The buckskin raised her head, ears pointing to the Yellow House Trail. Rance ignored her and watched the camp.

"If there was a lot of shooting here, they'd probably come back, and I could scoot out on this trail." He grinned and nudged his buckskin onto the trail.

Four Comancheros and a band of horses met
"*Yaaa!*" jumped his mare onto the trail.

"*Yaaa!*" Rance reined back in surprise.

His yell told the riders that he was gringo. They swung their carbines.

Bullets clipped leaves from the trees. One ricocheted from a limb as Rance spurred the mare to escape. He heard the whine of the ricochet as she leaned into a turn that hid them from the Comancheros.

He felt his back muscles tighten and rolled his shoulders to relax. A bead of perspiration itched his scalp.

Two Comancheros left the horse band and followed Rance on the trail. Their gunfire was wild and sporadic.

He sat low in his saddle, as his buckskin ran and he swayed to dodge the slash of mesquite limbs.

Still, he felt the whiplike sting of some. A ricochet ripped a tree limb. Splinters showered him as his mare followed a turn in the trail.

The firing stopped but the riders were gaining.

If I can get to the trail ahead of the big bunch of Comancheros, I'll have a chance to get away, he thought. They'll have to stop and explain what happened.

The larger group of Comancheros rode at a canter and Rance could hear them. The confused sounds of their voices, as they heard the shots, carried over the pounding run of his buckskin. The trails will join soon, he thought. He leaned down and patted the mare's neck. "We can't stop now." He touched her flanks with his spurs.

"Eyahaa! Get going."

The mare jumped from her canter into a pounding run that carried them onto the main trail ahead of the Comancheros.

Their horses reared in surprise, and the Comancheros hesitated before kicking them into a gallop. Confusion vanished as the raiders settled into pursuit of Rance.

He twisted in his saddle and watched the pursuing riders. "Damn, I thought they'd stop and palaver." His eyes showed concern as he looked at his buckskin. "I don't want you to run too much, but you're going to have to belly down for a while longer."

The Comancheros pushed their horses, but the buckskin was out of reach. They reined to a stop and gathered around the leader.

Rance slowed and watched, and three of the riders

spurred their horses after him. The others followed at a canter.

I don't like it, he thought. They can wear me down if they start relaying me. He watched the trail for a cutoff. There'll be one up ahead that'll get me to Laura's, and if Joe and his men are there, we can have a real set-to.

The three riders were gaining.

His buckskin began to lather.

"We won't make it."

A narrow trail that angled down and through a heavy stand of mesquite was the cutoff that Rance wanted. He wheeled his mare onto the trail that threaded itself between boulders and thick clumps of mesquite.

He could hear the riders as they followed. The trail worked its way up a ridge and dropped into a shallow ravine. As he topped the ridge, the riders began firing at him. Bullets ricocheted in spranging whines.

Beyond the ridge, he reined the mare to a stop, unbooted his carbine and ran back to a boulder beside the trail. A Comanchero was jumping his horse up the trail as Rance reached the boulder.

He squeezed the trigger as his sight settled on the man.

Levering as recoil threw the muzzle up, Rance settled his sight on the second rider before the first man had slipped from his saddle.

He stumbled, fell, and held his hand over the wound in his side.

The second rider's body rocked with his horse as it humped its way up the trail.

His shot missed, and as the man rolled out of his saddle for the shelter of dense mesquite that lined the trail, Rance's second bullet ripped the Comanchero's shoulder.

The raider's boot caught in his stirrup. His horse dragged him and kicked. The dragged man's face and chest were crushed before his boot came free.

The third rider had slipped into the trees that lined the trail. His horse stood and waited.

Rance crouched, watched the trail and listened.

Birds scratching for food, sounds of the Comancheros in the distance, and a rustling in the underbrush interrupted the quiet.

He listened intently to the rustling and an occasional ring of a spur rowel. The ridge where he waited was open, and only tall grass and rock rubble covered the clearing. His back muscles were tensed and his eyes searched for the third rider.

A mesquite tree below him jerked abruptly, and across the trail another waved in the breeze that had come up.

A rock rolled near the ridge, and Rance turned and swung his carbine as he heard a shot. Its ricochet ripped the boulder by his head and rock chips sliced at his face. His carbine recoiled and its bullet chewed at the place where the Comanchero had been.

The raider rolled to his feet and levered his carbine into a rolling explosion that chewed at the boulder and ground around Rance.

He reeled back as rock dust and splinters showered him. Tripping on a rock, he fell and rolled. He came to his knees, leveled the carbine and fired.

He levered and fired a second shot.

The Comanchero swayed back, his body arced forward as if to embrace himself. He refused to fall and straightened.

Rance fired.

What had been the man's Adam's apple became a hole that bulged his neck. His legs collapsed and he fell forward, head hanging with an unnatural twist.

Rance took a deep breath, sighed and came to his feet. "I'd better go find Joe and his cowboys. If I'm going to stop Tafoya, I'll need all the help I can get."

11

Rance looked into the muzzle of a carbine when his buckskin cantered into the clearing at Laura's. "Whoa! Wait up," he called. "Take it easy with the gun."

"Mister," the man sighting on him said, "you ride slow and easy over to the corral or there won't be enough left of you to feed the buzzards."

Rance nodded and walked his mare toward the corral where a small fire burned. The back of his neck felt cold, and he rode the mare with a tight rein. If she starts frisking, he thought, he'll kill me for sure.

Two cowboys were squatted around the fire, and as the man followed Rance to the corral, they stood. "What have you got, Frank?"

"Comanchero, I figure." He gestured with the carbine. "Gunbelts across his chest."

"No," Rance argued as he dismounted. "I'm Rance Long Roper." He looked quickly at the three men. My name won't help, he thought. "I'm not a Comanchero. I came here to meet Joe Williams."

"Joe don't associate with Comancheros." The man with the carbine ignored Rance's denial and whirled him around. "Don't you lie to us." His craggy face glowered at Rance. "Bill Swanson here works with Joe." He turned to Bill. "Did you ever see this galoot before?"

Bill shook his head. "Stranger to me."

Rance's eyes narrowed as he watched the three men. He tried to shift his back away from them, but Frank pushed him near the fire.

"How did you know about Joe Williams? He's supposed to be here and he ain't. Did you bushwhack him?"

"Hell no, I didn't." He could feel anger boiling in his gut. I can't get mad, he thought. It'd be a mistake and I'd be dead.

"You know about him. Does Tafoya have a bunch of his raiders waiting out there?"

"Dammit!" Rance snapped, "I'm trying to stop Tafoya before he starts raiding any more than he has."

"One man stop Tafoya?" A tall lanky man across the fire looked curiously at Rance and laughed. "Do you figure to stop Tafoya?"

"I figure to try." Rance turned and glared at Frank. "If you push me again, I'll feed that carbine to you."

Frank's head came down, his eyes narrowed, and he moved toward Rance.

Rance settled on the balls of his feet, his thumb curled around the hammer of the Smith and Wesson. It cleared leather and cocked as he pointed. He jabbed the sixgun into Frank's gut and swiveled himself and Frank around. "If either of you try anything funny, you'll be burying Frank."

"Wait up!" the tall lanky man said. "I know you. It was hard to remember, but I saw you at Bent's Fort when you had a set-to with a wolfer."

Rance pushed the .44 firmly into Frank's stomach and looked closely at the man. He nodded. "There was some trouble," he said grimly.

"Slim, you keep out of this," Frank ordered. "If he wants to shoot me," he looked into Rance's eyes, "have at it. I ain't crawling."

"I don't want you to do a damn thing except leave me be," he snapped. "I rode in here peaceful like to meet Joe, and you took after me like some sore ass steer."

"If you dress like a Comanchero, you got to figure someone will get hardnosed about it." Bill cleared his throat and spit.

"He's right," Slim agreed.

"You're wearing them gunbelts like one of Tafoya's Comancheros," Bill added.

Rance looked down at the gunbelts hanging from his shoulders and across his body. He shook his head and grinned. "Damn me, I forgot them."

"You ain't a Comanchero?" Frank looked from Rance to the others.

Rance shook his head.

Slim and Bill agreed. "Look at his horse. He don't have the trappings of a Comanchero."

"But you sure looked like one." Bill laughed uncomfortably.

"I'm sorry about that." Frank shook his head. "You can't be too careful these days."

"You're—" Slim interrupted himself to listen. He stood and walked away from the fire, tilted his head and looked at the others.

"What is it?" Frank watched Slim curiously. "You hear something?"

Slim nodded. "Listen. Running horses." He returned to the fire and took his carbine. As he levered a cartridge into the chamber, the others stood.

"I hear it." Bill took his carbine and walked to the corner of Laura's boarded-up store.

They scattered around the clearing as the sounds became louder.

Frank waited near the trail. He crouched and motioned for them to take cover.

Rance glanced at Slim waiting near a clump of scrub cedar, Bill relaxed at the corner of the store, and Frank squatted beside the trail. I'll wait here and see what happens, he decided, and settled himself beside the fire.

The sounds of running horses became louder. He could see a roll of dust on the trail and the men through breaks in the tree mass.

"Get cover, damnit," Frank called.

"Somebody's got to be at this fire." Rance squatted with the fire at his back, began to roll a cigarette, lighted it and lifted his carbine. He watched the dust as it neared and checked the loads in his carbine.

The Comancheros streamed into the clearing and reined to a stop.

Rance stood and butted the carbine to his hip as dust swirled in the clearing.

"Gringo!" A rider snarled the word and reined his horse near Rance. He laughed as his horse reared and he leaned forward to spit in Rance's face.

He stood and waited. As the man leaned forward, Rance lowered the carbine to point and pushed it in the man's face. He cocked the hammer and waited.

The rider's eyes widened. *"Madre de Dios!"* He straightened and Rance followed with the carbine still in his face. He glanced at the riders and back to the man looking into the muzzle of his carbine.

They knew what he would do if anyone tried to shoot him. The Comancheros sat their saddles until a voice broke the silence.

"Long Roper! It's Long Roper." Billy Joe's voice was excited. "Tafoya. There's your gringo."

Rance heard the sixgun cock. He squeezed the trigger and, as the rider's body was twisted back, hunkered behind the Comanchero's horse. The horse reared as its rider rolled out of his saddle, and gunfire racketed in the clearing. Smoke billowed and swirled around the riders. Horses reared and whinnied as Frank, Slim, and Bill began firing.

A corral railing splintered. A bullet whined into a ricochet. Dust puffs splashed his legs as Rance found a target.

A Comanchero sagged in his saddle but clung to his horse. He grasped the horn as his horse whirled and galloped out of the clearing.

Rance remembered where the sound of Billy Joe's voice had come from. He levered and stepped away from the shelter of the riderless horse, his carbine searching.

Billy Joe's horse reared as the two men saw the other. Rance pointed the carbine, his front sight settled on Billy Joe and he squeezed.

119

Billy Joe's horse reared, Rance's bullet ripped through its head, it humped its back and collapsed on its withers. As his horse rolled, Billy Joe scrambled away.

Rance moved toward him.

The horse attempted to stand and blocked his sight. It rolled, kicked and lay still.

His eyes searched hungrily for Billy Joe. Smoke hung thick in the clearing, and as Tafoya's Comancheros wheeled their horses in confusion, Rance saw him mount the dead Comanchero's horse and race out of the clearing.

Riders streamed onto the trail and out of the clearing.

He sighed. "Missed again."

Frank walked to the fire, and as Slim and Bill joined them, he turned to Rance. "I'll ride with you all the way. I sure figured you wrong."

"They were mounted, and it's hard to do good shooting when you're on a horse." He glanced away. "Looks like we've got some burying to do."

"There's a ravine over there." Slim pointed. "If we drag the horse into the ravine, the buzzards will take care of the rest."

"I sure don't like killing horses."

"It wasn't your fault, and it couldn't be helped." Slim turned. "Laura always kept a shovel out back. I'll try to find it, and we can bury the two Comancheros. It'll keep us busy till Joe gets here." He paused. "Someone ought to say a word over them."

"I will," Frank said.

Joe Williams reined to a stop near the fire and dismounted.

"What kept you?" Frank made room by the fire.

"There's a young feller and his family running cows on a little spread south of Garvey's. I thought he should be warned. No reason to get here any sooner." He looked at Frank. "Was there any trouble?"

"Not that you'd know." He smiled wistfully. "It gave us a chance to get acquainted with Rance."

"Good." He turned to Rance. "Do you have any ideas for stopping Tafoya?"

"Some." He rolled a cigarette, pinched the end and lighted it. "About five of the raiders are guarding a passel of stock at Tule Canyon, and the rest of his men are staying at Ledbetter's camp. At least it looks that way."

"What do you figure?"

"We ought to raid Tule Canyon and get the stock back, then maybe visit Tafoya."

"He's got a lot of men," Bill pointed out.

"Just five of us," Slim added.

"There wasn't too many at the Alamo, and they took on Santa Anna."

"And they're all dead."

"There's more ways to skin a cat. Sam Houston did it at San Jacinto."

"Do you figure to be like Sam Houston?" A grin creased Slim's face.

"No," Rance answered in mock seriousness. "He had some good men."

121

Frank laughed and turned to Joe. "We ought to prove to Rance that we're as good."

"Well, let's go stop Tafoya." Joe stood as Frank began to kill the fire. "I almost forgot." He turned to Rance. "Sue Garvey was asking about you."

Rance grinned and turned his head.

Tule Canyon lay in the shade of an afternoon sun. The five men watched Tafoya's camp from a ledge above Yellow House Trail.

"There should be five men," Rance said.

"I can see four." Slim shifted his position. "There's the fifth man. See him? Down by the corral."

"I can see him now." Rance nodded. He turned to Frank. "You thought I was a Comanchero?"

He nodded.

"Then maybe they will." Rance grinned wryly.

"I did, but I'm not a Comanchero." Frank tilted his head at Rance. "What are you planning?"

"We know where the five raiders are, so the trails around the camp are clear." He raised and settled his gunbelt. "Three of you can skirt the camp, and I'll take one of you and go into the camp from here. When we start into the camp, the three of you attract their attention, then come in hell bent for election."

"Like I said, I'm not a Comanchero. If they get you and beat us off, you won't even make good coyote bait."

"You're right, but Sam Houston didn't worry about it, and I sure as hell ain't."

"I think it'll work." Joe stepped on his cigarette. "Who do you want with you?"

"How about you, Frank?"

"You damn right. I want to see this close up."

"I'll take Bill and Slim," Joe said. "Give us ten minutes, and we'll put on a good show."

Joe led them along the trail that skirted the camp. He slowed as they neared the trail to Fort Worth. He turned to Slim. "You know these trails, Slim. Is this the one that would take us to the Adobe Walls Trail?"

"Right." Slim nodded. "It's wide and straight. If we get the horses, this is the trail we should use."

"Stay here," Joe ordered. "I want to check the trail." He nudged his horse onto the trail and suddenly wheeled back. "Comancheros!" he warned.

"How many?"

"About ten." His face grew solemn. "They'll get Frank and Rance."

"We've got to stop them."

"Slim," Joe ordered, "I'll get across the trail, and with Bill on this side, we can hold them off long enough for you to warn Rance and Frank."

"No," Slim argued. "You'll need—"

"Shut up," Joe interrupted. "When I get across the trail, you shag your ass up to the camp."

"That's right," Bill added. "They're depending on us to do a little tail twisting."

"Then you get across," Slim snapped.

"Wait till we slow them down." He wheeled his horse and jumped it across the trail.

Slim could hear the startled yells of the Coman-cheros and Joe's carbine as it punctuated their angry calls. Horses whinnied and squealed.

Bill crouched by the trail and began firing.

Slim lay his spurs on his horse and leaned into its jumping lunge that carried him onto the trail. Dust swirled into a roll that followed Slim. A bullet splintered a mesquite limb, another ricocheted from a rock as he leaned into a turn in the trail.

Sporadic gunfire settled into occasional shots as the raiders retreated along their backtrail.

Rance and Frank ambled their horses toward the camp.

"Stay slouched back against your cantle," Rance said.

"I know. Boots forward, stiff-legged."

Rance grinned and nodded.

"Do you know any of that Mexican lingo?"

"I know amigo, but not much more." Rance looked back at Frank. "Just nod and grin is about all we can do." His smile was washed out.

The sounds of gunfire interrupted him.

"What the hell's that?" Frank straightened.

"They ran into trouble." He looked across the hills.

"Someone's pounding leather up this way," Frank added. "See that dust?"

Rance turned and watched the camp.

Three raiders around the fire stood, waved at Rance, and watched the trail. Two Comancheros ran from the corral to camp.

"They waved to us, and they're watching the trail," Rance said. "While they're watching, let's bust in and get the horses and cattle out of the corral."

"Get going." Frank unbooted his carbine.

As the two raiders reached the fire, Rance spurred his buckskin into a run, drew his sixgun and thumbed a shot at the five men.

Frank's carbine went into action.

The fire exploded in a shower of sparks. The raiders reeled away from the flying sparks, hot coals, and burning splinters as Frank and Rance pounded through the camp. One man ran toward them.

Frank's boot caught him in the face.

Rance hit the ground running as his buckskin slowed, and he dumped the gate railings as Frank spurred his horse into the corral.

"*Eyahaa!*" Frank's yell caused the horses and cattle to snort and mill.

Rance dropped to his knees and began firing at the five men scrambling for their guns.

Slim jumped his horse onto the trail and reined to a stop when he saw Rance and Frank at the corral.

"*Eyahaa!*" Slim waved and unbooted his carbine. "*Eyahaa*, Stampede!*"

"*Eyahaa!*" Frank waved as he hazed the stock toward the raider's camp.

"Run 'em, goddammit. Run 'em," Rance yelled at Frank and he swung into his saddle.

The horses running ahead of the cattle were through the camp before the raiders were able to clear. A man ran across the trail, he tripped and fell ahead of the horses.

The cattle followed and they chewed the camp into

a soggy mess.

Slim waited on the trail. He untied his poncho and, as the horses neared, he began to wave.

The horses were without a leader. They slowed and began to mill.

Slim swore at them and waved the poncho.

A dun mare shook her head and wheeled onto the trail Slim had used.

"Eyahaa!" Slim's yell panicked the horses and they followed the mare. The stampeding cattle thundered toward the horses. They slowed, crowded the horses and, as they streamed onto the trail, the cattle followed.

Rance and Frank reined their horses to a canter as they followed the cattle.

"You sure ripped that camp apart," Slim yelled.

Rance laughed and looked back.

A man walked out of the trees and shook his fist at them.

"Where's Joe and Bill?" Rance asked.

"They're standing off about ten Comancheros on down the trail."

"Then let's stampede this stock right down through them."

Slim laughed.

12

Over the sounds of stock on the trail, Rance could hear gunfire. He swiveled in the saddle. "Frank, it sounds like Joe and Bill are still kicking."

Frank grinned. "I figure so." He glanced over his shoulder. "What about those raiders we left at Tule Canyon?"

"I've been thinking about them." Rance looked back along the trail. "If they don't try to get the stock back, Tafoya'll probably nail their hides to the barn door."

"You want me to drop back and keep a watch out for them?"

"No. The two of you can handle stock better than me." He reined up. "I'll go back and watch for them."

"Are you sure?" Frank watched Rance wheel his horse.

"When you get close to the Comancheros," he called back, "stampede them." Rance cantered his buckskin along the trail until he could see beyond the turn of their backtrail, then reined the mare to a stop and waited.

The trail was quiet and empty except for a jack

rabbit that scooted across. Rising above the crowding tops of mesquite, the Caprock, a broken rocky wall that edged the Panhandle, sat dark and foreboding. The afternoon sun was hidden by heavy clouds that were building for a storm.

It's going to rain on the Panhandle, he thought, and we might get some down here. Seems like it'll never stop, and I'm damn tired of sleeping in a wet bed every time it rains. He rolled a cigarette and lighted it. I'm going to find me a place around here and maybe marry Miss Sue. He grinned. There's nothing wrong with that.

A band of horsemen appeared around a turn in the trail. A roll of dust trailed them and hung in the air.

Looks like five riders, he thought. Probably the Comancheros from Tule Canyon. He unbooted the carbine and swung out of his saddle.

The buckskin tossed her head.

He jerked the reins. "Ho, girl. Don't get frisky." Rance led her to the side of the trail and dallied the reins on a mesquite limb. "You stay out of sight while I slow them down."

The riders were closer. He could see them clearly and nodded. About right, he thought. I can warn them and still have time if they don't stop. He jacked a cartridge into the chamber.

The exploding sound of his carbine startled a jack rabbit that scooted across the trail and disappeared into the trees.

Dust puffed a ricochet on the trail.

The riders slowed.

Rance looked over his shoulder at Frank and Slim. Frank waved and they began hazing the cattle and horses into a run that carried them around a turn in the trail.

Rance drew back as a volley of shots raised puffs of dust near him.

The raiders trotted their horses along the trail and slowed to a walk when Rance didn't return their fire.

He waited.

One of the raiders gestured, and a horseman spurred his horse into a gallop.

Rance settled himself, slowly pointed the carbine and fired a shot that threw up dust ahead of the horse. Recoil raised the muzzle. He levered a cartridge into the chamber, and as the raider began firing, he squeezed the trigger.

The Comanchero's arm came up, and he rolled out of his saddle. His body bounced, skidded and twisted into a formless heap. Dust swirled around the still form.

The four riders kicked their horses into a charge.

Rance began firing.

A rider clutched his arm. A second man sagged in his saddle and reined his horse away. The two remaining riders discovered themselves alone, reined to a stop, wheeled their horses and followed the others.

He relaxed and began to thumb cartridges into the carbine's magazine. Maybe they'll stay at Tule, he thought.

The mare snorted as he took the reins and legged himself into the saddle, slipped the carbine into its boot and nudged her onto the trail.

Frank swiveled in his saddle as Rance slowed to a walk. "Did you stop them?"

He nodded. "How far ahead are Joe and Bill?"

"Slim thinks it's around that turn up ahead."

"I remember that busted mesquite." Slim pointed.

"We're close enough to stampede them."

Frank grinned. "Let's get at it."

"*Eyahaa!*" Slim's yell sounded happy and wild. It echoed across the mesquite and along the trail as cattle and horses raised their heads and began to trot.

Rance rump-popped a steer with his rope as Frank fired over their heads.

Thunder rumbled beyond the Caprock, and a flurry of raindrops raised puffs of dust on the trail.

The cattle bawled and broke into a run as they rounded a turn in the trail. Needle sharp horns prodded the horses. A few kicked at the steers, but all of the horses jumped into a run ahead of them.

Thunder broke overhead, and lightning ripped the rapidly darkening sky.

Rance could see saddled horses tied to trees along the trail. Men suddenly materialized beside their horses, their faces white in the sudden flash of lightning. As they wheeled their horses ahead of the stampeding herd, the light shower became a heavy rain.

Rance and the two men shrugged into their slickers as they pounded by the waiting Joe and Bill.

Rance reined up and, as Slim and Frank wheeled back to join him, looked down at Joe. "Are you and Bill all right?"

"We got tired of waiting, but that's the worst."

Joe stepped onto his saddle and slipped into his slicker. He nodded toward Bill. "He's madder than a sore-tailed steer."

"What's wrong?" Rance turned.

"Them damn Comancheros." Bill glowered at the trail. "One of them tried to kill me. Split a mesquite limb right by my head."

Joe laughed.

"The stock's getting away," Rance interrupted and spurred his buckskin into a gallop ahead of the others.

The trail had turned into a river. Their horses threw up sprays of mud and rainwater. And as they galloped after the herd, a slash of lightning ended in a roll of thunder. The thunder sounded different. It had the hard flat sound of a carbine.

Rance heard the sound and felt a tug at his slicker. A bullet had ripped at the hook. His yell of surprise choked in his throat as he reined back. The buckskin attempted to stop and lost her footing.

"Raiders!" He called a warning as the mare twisted and fell. Rance had his booted foot up and, as the mare rolled, stepped away from her and whirled to face the bushwhacker. His sixgun was up searching for a target.

Frank appeared beside him and looked down. His hat spilled water on the trail. "Are you all right?"

He nodded and walked to the buckskin as she scrambled to her feet. Rain swirled around him as the wind gusted and soaked his already wet clothing.

Bill and Slim reined to the side of the trail. They rode slowly, carbines ready as they examined the trees. Sheeting rain blinded them, but they tugged at their hat brims to shield their eyes.

As Rance swung into his saddle, he heard the sudden sound of Bill and Slim's carbines.

Joe joined Frank and Rance. They watched the two men wheel away from the trees.

"Okay?"

They nodded. Slim pointed to the stock. "We've got to pen them up somewhere," he called.

"There's a clearing that'll hold them on the other side of the turnoff to Ledbetter's camp."

"We better get them to that clearing. They're getting all red-eyed and raunchy."

"Let's go." Rance spurred his buckskin.

"Watch out for bushwhackers," Frank warned.

Rance nodded. "Check every clearing. We don't want them sneaking up on our backside."

A mesquite limb splintered beside Frank. His carbine swung, pointed, and he fired.

Rance and the others fired as Frank's carbine recoiled. Rance levered and fired a second time as the squat outline of a man scrambled onto his horse and raced away.

The cattle were nervous. The horses whinnied and tossed their heads as they moved ahead of the cattle.

Rance heard a shot. Three carbines ripped the darkness.

Bullets ricocheted away or splashed up a spray of water.

The cattle bawled. They wanted to run and began to push the horses ahead of them.

Lightning broke over the Caprock and slashed at

the heavy clouds overhead. Thunder rolled angrily and ended with an explosive clap across the sky.

The cattle and horses began to run. Rain pounded their backs. It sheeted on the trail.

Comancheros scrambled to their horses. A rider was caught in the crush of cattle. A longhorn steer ripped at the rider's horse. The Comanchero screamed as his horse rolled under the crush of half-wild cattle.

"They're getting away," Frank called.

"Let them go. They won't stop in this rain." Rance shielded his eyes from the rain and glanced at Frank as he heard a carbine shot.

Frank's body twisted and swayed. He tried to raise his arm.

Spurring his buckskin, Rance moved to his side. "Is it bad?"

He shook his head. "My shoulder." He grimaced with pain. "Missed the bone. I'll be all right."

"Are you sure?"

He nodded. "We're losing the cattle."

"Let them go," Rance said. "We've got to find a place to hole up."

They turned to see the dark silhouetted form of Joe materialize beside them. "I looked for the horses a minute ago. They've vanished and the cattle are running." He looked at Frank. "You've been hit."

Frank nodded and grinned wryly. "Those longhorns'll clean this trail all the way to Childress's place. We won't need to worry about Comancheros after them steers are through."

"I'm worrying about a place to camp." Rance

133

studied the sky. "The rain's settling in for the night."

"Past the turnoff there's a lean-to in a bois d'arc clearing. It ain't big, but we can squeeze in." Joe stretched his back muscles.

As Rance watched, Joe's mouth opened with a gasp. His body was thrown forward.

"Ahaaa . . ."

Rance heard the carbine. The sound came from their backtrail.

"Slim! Bill!" Frank called. "Joe's been hit."

Rance swung out of the saddle, and as Bill and Slim appeared beside them, he motioned them along the trail. "You get Joe to the clearing. I'm going to get me a bushwhacker."

"You'll need help." Slim started to dismount.

"Goddammit, get your ass to that clearing. Joe needs you more than me."

"Rance knows what he's doing." Frank motioned to Slim. "Let's get Joe to the clearing."

He watched as they wheeled their horses and moved down the trail. Their hoofs made sucking sounds in the mud as Rance splashed his way to the trees that lined the trail.

The sounds of Frank and the others faded into the steady sound of rain on the trail, as Rance dallied the buckskin's reins to a mesquite and crouch-walked away from the mare.

I should be able to hear him, he thought. Levering a cartridge into the carbine's chamber, he squatted beside the trail and waited.

The rain eased, but with a clap of thunder it began to sheet, and he strained his eyes to see. A trickle of

134

water edged around the sweatband of his hat and ran down the back of his neck. The flannel shirt clung to his shoulders and back. His hands were wet, and he tried to dry them. I can't take a chance on their slipping, he thought.

Lightning brightened the sky over the Caprock. Three horsemen appeared on the trail slowly walking their horses toward Rance. They vanished as the darkness returned with a roll of thunder.

"Oh damn. My hands are wet." He threaded his gun hand under the waistband of his pants and wiped it dry. Holding the carbine tucked under his slicker, he tried to dry the lever and stock.

Slow plodding sounds of the riders' horses seemed loud. He eased his gun hand to the carbine, slowly cocked the hammer and strained his eyes to see the trail. Rain spilled from his hat brim as he turned his head.

Three slickered riders appeared on the trail. Distant lightning gleamed on the folds of their oilskin slickers. Their faces were hidden, but he knew they were studying the trail.

As he slowly raised the carbine to point, lightning speared the sky. It reflected from the barrel.

A Comanchero grunted a warning and brought his carbine around.

Rance pointed, fired and levered into a blunt, hard-rolling sound that blasted the air.

The muzzle flash of his carbine showed a raider rolling out of his saddle and another reeling back.

He continued to fire and moved to the center of the trail. His gunfire lashed the standing rainwater into a spray. He paused and waited.

A horse snorted. A flash of lightning showed three horses standing heads down, their saddles empty.

He shook his head sadly. "It's sure hard scratching, but nothing comes easy," he mumbled and began to reload the carbine. "I'd better see how Joe is."

13

Rance recognized the turnoff to Ledbetter's camp. The twisted limb of a bois d'arc had caught his hat, he remembered. He slowed his buckskin, stopped and stepped down from the saddle. Leading his mare to the side, he tied her reins to a limb and catwalked to the entrance.

A horse drooped its head beneath a tall bois d'arc where its slickered rider had squatted and attempted to light a cigarette.

Only one guard, he thought. He swiveled and studied the trail. It was dreary, wet and gray. The trees had lost their shapes in the haze of a heavy rain. I think I can get past the opening if I lead the mare, he thought. He turned back to the guard.

The squatting man had angrily thrown his soggy cigarette away and patiently began to roll another.

Rance returned to the buckskin and rubbed her neck.

She shook her head.

"Now you keep quiet. I don't want him to see us." He led her across the trail and carefully followed it near the trees.

Distant lightning flashed, but he was hidden in

the tree shadows. Past the opening, he drew the mare to him and mounted. If that was the only man watching, we're all right, he decided. There could have been another one that I didn't see. He sourly glanced over his shoulder.

As Rance's buckskin carried him around a turn in the trail, a slickered rider walked his horse onto the trail from the cutoff. He rode slowly, his vaquero slouch merging with the trees.

Rance looked along his backtrail and shook his head. "Something's wrong," he growled to himself. "I don't know what it is, but something's wrong."

The rain swirled and buffeted him as the wind picked up. Mesquite trees whipped wildly with the wind, and broken limbs tumbled and skittered across the trail.

His buckskin nervously whinnied and shook her head. Rance reined to a stop and swiveled in his wet saddle. He studied shadows along the trail, shadows that became stunted mesquite and bois d'arc. I'm getting jumpy. Maybe I'm seeing things, but that looked like a rider just sitting there. Damn me, I must be seeing things. He nudged the buckskin into a walk.

The mare snorted as her hoofs splashed through puddles of rainwater.

The indistinct form of Slim spilled water from his hat as he raised his head. "Rance!" His words were quiet and urgent. "Keep going. There's a rider behind you."

He straightened with a start, nodded and nudged the mare. His back muscles drew tight, and he could feel the ripple of tension that ran up his back. He leaned forward and patted the mare's neck. "Easy, girl. Just keep walking." Glancing back, he could see the indistinct form that was a horseman.

A carbine shot sounded muffled and distant.

Lightning brightened the trail. It highlighted a horse waiting, its rider crumpled on the trail.

Rance wheeled back and, as he reined to a stop, Slim was pushing the body of a lifeless rider onto the empty saddle and lashing it down.

"Let them bury him," he said bluntly.

"How's Joe and Frank?"

"Frank's patched up. He'll be all right."

"Joe?"

Slim looked up and shook his head. "Gone." He motioned with his head. "Go on in. The lean-to's on the left." He slapped the rump of the Comanchero's horse.

It jumped and trotted back along the trail as Rance led his buckskin into the clearing.

The lean-to was dry, warmed by a small fire hidden from the trail. Bill shifted his place by the fire for Rance. Frank looked up and smiled wistfully.

"It ain't been the best of days." His voice was low. He sounded tired.

Rance nodded as he shed his slicker.

"Is Slim coming in?"

"He figures there'll be more riders on the trail. The clouds are breaking up, and you can see a few stars."

"I'll go out and relieve him when I finish this coffee." Bill averted his eyes. "I'm sure sorry, Rance."

"For what?" He looked closely at Bill.

"We sort of let you down."

"Hell now," he growled. His tired face saddened. "You didn't let anyone down. Joe's dead." He paused and swallowed with difficulty. "And Frank's been winged. If there was any letting down, it was me."

Frank held his cup for Bill to pour more coffee. "I think everybody's feeling sorry for themselves, and there's no need for that."

"You're probably right." Rance fingered his shirt pocket for tobacco and papers. "I know this much, no one's riding with me anymore. I'm settling with Billy Joe by myself."

"What about Tafoya and Ledbetter?"

"They come next, but I'm not going to have someone else killed because of me. Not like Joe." A tear edged itself to the corner of his eye and ran down his cheek.

"You've got no right to figure it's just your fight. There's others who've got a reason to fight."

"That may be, but I'm making it mine, and that's the only reason I need." He lighted his cigarette.

A horse snorted in the clearing.

The three men turned to face the sound. As Rance slipped into the clearing, Bill and Frank moved away from the fire, guns drawn.

Rance quietly drifted across the clearing to where Slim waited.

"Slim," he whispered, "it's me, Rance. We heard a horse. What happened?"

"Not much. I think one of our horses heard that coyote that yelped over across the hills."

"Is anyone on the trail?"

"I saw one rider down a ways, but he turned and went the other way."

"Damn." Rance shook his head. "If one of them is moving around, there'll be others, and they might come this way. Keep an eye out."

"I will."

"I want you to know what I told Frank and Bill."

Slim looked at him curiously.

"As soon as things look good, I want Bill to take Joe back to the ranch. You and Frank go back to the Matador. You've done more'n enough."

"The hell you say."

"Nobody else is going to be killed on my account."

"I didn't figure he was." Slim flicked a raindrop from his nose. "We came out here to try and stop Tafoya. It wasn't because you needed help, so don't start feeling biggity about it." He grinned.

"It was my idea to raid Tule Canyon and bring the stock up this trail."

"And Joe and Bill's idea to stand off the raiders, and me to come and warn you and Frank. It ain't nobody's fault. It just happened."

Rance gripped Slim's arm.

They moved away from the opening as the splashing of a horse's hoofs sounded near. A rider appeared on the trail as he moved past the opening.

"They're out looking."

Slim nodded. "What's your plans?"

"The only plans I have are for all of you to scoot out of here."

Slim turned as Bill appeared at their sides. "They're on the trail." He gestured with his head and spoke quietly. "Looking for us."

o get some coffee, you too, Rance. I'll watch."
settled by a bois d'arc and studied the trail.

Rance followed Slim to the lean-to and settled himself across the fire from Slim.

"Rance figures he wants to hog all the glory by being a lone wolf." Slim raised the cup to his lips. His face was emotionless as he watched Rance.

"I work better that way."

"Sure can't fault you for that," Frank said. "But you're a drifter. When it's over and done with, you'll be gone. Most of us are figuring on settling down around here, and we've got a stake in stopping Tafoya."

"I figure on settling around here if I can find a place." A sudden smile broke the solemness of his face. "I might start courting and get married."

Frank started to smile, but he turned suddenly.

Loud voices came from the trail.

Bill appeared in the lean-to. "They're coming into this clearing. Hear them?"

Frank nodded. "Sounds like whoever's honchoing that bunch wants all the riders with him."

"They'll see the fire and investigate," Rance said. "If they do and we're in the trees at the edge of the clearing, the fire will skylight them. They'll make good targets."

"Let's go," Frank said abruptly. "We ain't got much time before they'll be in the clearing."

The four men slipped out of the lean-to and melted into the darkness.

Rance catwalked to the opening that led to the trail. He waited, crouched beneath a bois d'arc.

A horseman jumped his horse into the clearing, a

carbine swinging in his hand. Others followed and they cautiously circled the clearing. They studied the lean-to, the fire, and the still body of Joe lying in the shelter of the lean-to as if he were asleep.

The leader of the horsemen motioned with his hand, and the raiders converged on the lean-to.

Rance slipped along the edge of the opening, where he saw a single rider waiting on the trail. I can't do anything until Frank gives the signal, he thought. He returned to the clearing and waited for the signal.

A Comanchero glanced over his shoulder. He saw the reflection of Slim's carbine and gave a startled yell.

The raiders wheeled their horses.

Three carbines ripped the darkness.

The Comancheros' horses reared and whinnied.

Rance waited, and as a raider spurred his horse to escape, he squeezed the trigger. The carbine bucked its recoil. As the raider swayed crazily and rolled out of his saddle, Rance whirled and ran to the trail.

The man waiting on his horse had spurred it into a hard run as Rance pointed and fired.

His shot ricocheted away. He whirled and began firing at the Comancheros attempting to escape.

Horses reared and whinnied in fear.

The firing stopped. Gunsmoke drifted in the clearing.

Rance eased his way back into the clearing as Slim appeared beside him.

"We've got some prisoners," he said brightly. "Three dead, four winged, and three just didn't want to fight."

Frank walked across the clearing, shredding a veil of gunsmoke with his body. "What are we going to do with them?"

"Leave them be." Rance began to feed cartridges into the magazine of his carbine. "There was a rider on the trail. He got away, and every one of Tafoya's men will be down here faster'n you can shake a stick."

"Bill," Frank turned. "You get Joe out here and I'll get his horse. Move it. We don't have much time."

As Bill completed tying Joe's body on his saddle and mounted, the others were in their saddles and waiting.

"There's still enough clouds to hide the moon," Rance said. "Get going."

"Ain't you coming with us?" Frank turned.

"I've got something to do."

Slim twisted in his saddle and studied Rance curiously. "Are you loco?"

"Get going, dammit. They'll be down here before you know it." His words were pleading and urgent.

Frank nodded. "Take care of yourself." He waved and led them out of the clearing.

Rance followed, crossed the trail, and reined his buckskin to a stop back of bois d'arc. He turned and watched the three riders.

Slim looked back, watched Rance for a moment, then followed Frank.

They disappeared around a turn in the trail as Tafoya's Comancheros slowed their horses at the clearing and cautiously entered. Three men waited on the trail.

Rance waited and the buckskin turned her head and looked at him. He rubbed her neck as the three riders looked into the clearing.

Two of the riders shrugged and followed the others into the clearing. The third man settled in his saddle and waited.

Rance slipped out of his saddle and catwalked to the rider's side.

"Amigo." He gestured with the .44 as the man glanced down. "Down. Pronto."

The Comanchero's eyes widened and he eased himself to the ground.

Rance prodded him with the .44 and spun him around. As the Comanchero's hat fell, he lifted the sixgun and chopped.

The raider sighed and sprawled on the trail unconscious.

14

Rance left his buckskin near the trail to Ledbetter's camp. Under a tall bois d'arc in a clearing near the trail, he eased the cinch and worked his way back to a game trail he had discovered.

A full moon broke through the clouds. The game trail threaded its way around, through, and between clumps of trees in the thicket.

This could take me to the camp. He squatted and studied the trail where it twisted its way through the thicket. A few still dry spots showed the cloven hoofmarks of mule deer. If the mulies use it, I can get through.

A quick shower rattled the leaves overhead as he followed the game trail.

He heard quiet voices and a quick laugh. That's probably the guard. He paused and listened. Two of them, he decided. The tension of the fight was easing, and he rolled his shoulders. If Billy Joe's there, I'll pay my debt to Laura.

A chorus of frogs croaked in the thicket and over their sounds, he could hear distant voices. He paused and cocked his head to listen. Too hard to make out, he thought. I wouldn't know what they were saying anyway. If Billy Joe and Ledbetter are there, they'll talk plain English.

He crouched into a squat and sighed. If I find Billy Joe, I should just up and shoot him, but it'd stick in my craw. I've got to let him know I'm around, and then the whole damn camp'll know it. But I'll have to do it that way, and it'll have to be fast or I won't get out alive.

He raised from his crouch, heard a sound and spun around.

A knife flashed in the weak moonlight. It missed. A raider had lunged at him but tripped. He sprawled on the trail, scrambled and rolled to the side.

Rance tried to stomp the man's knife hand and missed.

In the dark tree shadows, the Comanchero was nearly hidden, and damp leaf litter on the ground deadened his sounds. Only an occasional scuffle of leaves warned Rance that he was waiting.

He crouched and watched the shadows. A bead of perspiration edged itself down his neck.

The knifeman moved slowly and cautiously. His eyes showed in the shadows, but his body merged into the darkness and became only a vague shape.

Rance watched his eyes. They'll tell me what he's going to do. I can't wait for him. I've got to do something. If I shoot, all hell will break loose.

Holding the knife under a fold of his serape, the raider eased himself toward Rance. He smiled at the thought of delivering the gringo to Tafoya. "Gringo," he snarled and lowered his body into a crouch.

Rance's hand moved to the twisted limb of a bois

d'arc. He shook the limb, stepped forward and kicked. His booted foot caught an exposed root.

The knife snaked out. It gleamed in the weak moonlight and slashed through Rance's shirt.

He felt the blade across his stomach. Anger boiled in his gut. It throbbed in his throat. His eyes narrowed, and he grunted under his breath.

The Comanchero watched as Rance moved toward him. He backed along the trail, eyes wide, suddenly afraid.

Rance touched his stomach and the blood. His temples pounded as the muscles in his neck swelled.

"You bastard," he growled and lunged.

The raider turned to run. His spur caught on a root and he tripped. Scrambling frantically, he rolled away as Rance leaped.

His booted feet landed on the man's back and, as the raider slashed blindly with his knife, Rance's hand went under the Comanchero's head, grasped his jaw and pulled. The man's shoulders raised, the knife slashed wildly as the air. Rance twisted his body and drove a knee between the Comanchero's shoulder blades. The knife plunged its point into the littered trail.

His body sagged, and Rance felt more than heard the sharp crack.

Backing away from the dead Comanchero, he sat on the trail. His hands were shaking and his body felt drawn and tight. He carefully probed the knife cut that had missed his stomach. It had cut across his rib cage, where his ribs had deflected the blade. His hand was covered with blood, and he wiped it on his pants.

If Billy Joe's there, he decided, I'll have to get this over with before I bleed too much. He turned and carefully moved along the game trail toward Ledbetter's camp. He could see the fires through the trees and slowed his approach.

Three fires were burning in the clearing and, near the river, a horse band cropped on the short grass.

Rance watched in the darkness and relaxed beside the twisted trunk of a bois d'arc. He slipped his Smith and Wesson from its holster and checked the cartridges. They gleamed dully in the moonlight. He slipped the sixgun into its holster and watched the clearing.

Huddled around two of the fires, seraped figures crouched, gestured and laughed. A few men relaxed beside the third fire. Ledbetter hunkered forward, and his eyes studied Tafoya who sat beside the fire. Both men were cautious and wary of the other.

It's not hard to know who's Ledbetter and Tafoya. He grinned. No love lost between them. Where's Billy Joe? He studied the men squatting around the fires and sourly decided that Billy Joe had left. Maybe he never was here, he thought. "Maybe I've just been wasting my time," he growled and turned his attention to Ledbetter and Tafoya. The Comanchero gestured as he spoke.

"Senor Ledbetter, your amigo Billy Joe, he is not here. Will he return?"

"I don't know where he is. He left yesterday and didn't say."

Tafoya shrugged. "My senora, she said bad." He glowered at the fire. "The gringo who stole my horses is the devil himself." He spit the words.

"I wish we could find him." Ledbetter rubbed his nose.

"If we do," Tafoya grinned evilly, "I have two mestizos who can cut out his heart and show it to him before he dies." His teeth flashed in a twisted smile. "Muerte."

Rance's grin faded as he listened. He won't get a chance if I can help it. I've had enough of knives, and before someone discovers that I'm here, he decided, I'd better get out. He carefully turned to leave.

A Comanchero stood from his place by the fire. He saw the dim figure of Rance, spoke to a man beside him and pointed. "Gringo!"

"Damn," Rance growled.

Tafoya came to his feet and whirled.

Ledbetter rolled to his feet and ran from the clearing. Two of his men followed.

Rance whirled to face the Comancheros. His .44 flashed in the dim light as he drew. Tafoya, he thought, and ran to the raider chief.

Tafoya started his draw but he stopped as Rance pointed his sixgun.

Two carbines exploded ricochets at him.

"*Alto! No bueno!*" Tafoya called as he watched Rance's sixgun point at him.

He stood beside Tafoya before any of the raiders could move, jabbed his .44 into the Comanchero's side and took his sixgun. He tossed it to the side.

"Gringo." Tafoya spit the word.

"Muerte," Rance said quietly. "You muerte." He roughly spun Tafoya around and backed away from the men. Ledbetter's out there somewhere with two others, he thought.

"Ledbetter," he called. "If you shoot me, Tafoya'll die and his men will tear you apart. The three of you get back by the fire."

The Comancheros moved restlessly.

"No!" Tafoya called to his men and his words carried the fear he felt.

The raiders waited and watched Tafoya for a sign of what to do.

"Tell them," Rance said. "Tell them to kill Ledbetter and his men if you are killed, and make it in English," he grinned, "so everybody will know."

Tafoya nodded. "The gringo Ledbetter," he said. His words carried in the clearing. "If I die, kill the gringo." His voice rose angrily. "All gringos!"

The clearing quieted as Tafoya spoke. Only the sounds of the fire broke the silence. A coyote called in the distance. The Comancheros moved restlessly, and their spur rowels rang like little bells.

"Ledbetter, you and your men get back here." Rance listened intently for the sound of anyone at his back.

A twig snapped. Silence.

His stomach drew into a knot, uncertainty pulled at his gut, and a bead of perspiration itched his scalp.

He moved his head to watch the edge of the clearing. A tree limb shook, and he twisted toward the sound.

The .44 bucked as he thumbed and fanned three shots.

A ricochet sounded. Splinters of wood showered the clearing.

A man coughed and gagged.

Tafoya broke to run.

"No!" Rance's word was abrupt and hard as he turned back.

The Comanchero stopped.

The crashing sound of a falling body sounded behind Rance.

"Back up." Rance's face hardened as he watched the clearing.

Tafoya's Comancheros stood quietly and waited as Ledbetter and his two men walked to the fire.

"Now amigo," Rance prodded with the .44, "we're going into the woods." He edged himself and Tafoya toward the game trail.

"Senor." Tafoya turned his head. "I have done what you want. You will not kill me?"

"No. I've got nothing against you as long as you get the hell out of this part of the country. I only want Billy Joe."

"I can get him for you."

"I want him alive." He pushed Tafoya along the trail and glanced over his shoulder.

"Si." Tafoya nodded anxiously. "I will bring him."

"Bring him?"

"Si."

"All right." Rance paused to listen. "The place where we had that little shooting, the store and corral?" Rance looked at the raider chief. What's he got in mind? Rance tilted his head and watched Tafoya. I might not be there, he thought, but it just might flush Billy Joe out of the woods.

"We will bring him there." Tafoya watched Rance anxiously.

"Alive?"

"Si."

"And you get out of the country?"

"Si, yes."

"Why should I trust you? You may be lying."

"Senor, I do not lie."

Rance didn't answer. His smile was sour.

They skirted the dead Comanchero. His knife gleamed dully on the trail. Rance stopped and spun Tafoya around.

"Tafoya, you listen close." He jabbed the gun in the Comachero's gut. "I'll be waiting at the clearing, and if you try anything I'll come after you."

Tafoya nodded quickly and shrugged as he watched Rance's eyes harden.

"This is far enough from camp. Get back to your men."

Rance whirled and ran to his buckskin. He cinched the saddle down and led his mare through the trees.

Loud voices and the pounding of horses' hoofs sounded in the clearing.

They'll be coming out of the clearing, and I've got to slow them down. He unbooted his carbine and ran to the turnoff. I wouldn't get halfway to the turn before they'd have me.

The guard had swung into his saddle as Rance appeared and fired at the rider. His horse reared and wheeled. He lost the reins, struggled to control his horse and slipped from the saddle, as his horse dodged away from a string of riders charging out of the clearing.

Rance fired, levered, fired, and levered his shots into a barrage.

The guard's riderless horse collided with another. A man was thrown from his saddle.

Horses reared and squealed.

Riders reined back and wheeled their horses.

Rance continued to fire into the confused mass of men and horses.

A Comanchero, thrown from his horse, ran toward Rance, a carbine in his hand.

Rance pointed and fired.

The Comanchero's booted feet twisted and folded under him. His carbine spun in the air as he plowed his face into the mud.

"I'd better get out of here," he grunted. "It'll take them a while to get untangled." He whirled and ran to his buckskin.

Rance booted his carbine as he wheeled the mare. He looked back at the turnoff, grinned and patted the buckskin's neck. "Maybe I can bed down at Missus Laura's in one of her shanties, and I'll get you some grain."

15

Ledbetter and his three men sat quietly by the fire. They glumly watched the big Comanchero pace the clearing like some restless animal.

"You are only bastard pigs!" He angrily glared at his men and stalked around the fire. His fury lashed at them. They stood hats in their hands and heads bowed. He tried to spit into the fire, but his mouth was dry from his anger. "Five gringos. Only five. You did not kill them." He spat the words angrily.

Ledbetter watched Tafoya and grinned sourly. "He's mad, real mad."

Cotton Resor nodded and looked at Ledbetter. His face, like an old boot, was splotched with marks of the pox he'd had as a kid, and his thin mouth was lifeless. He shifted his body uneasily. "If he comes after me like that, I'll kill him."

"There's too many of them for that," Vatch Green said quietly. His eyes, hidden under bushy eyebrows, reflected the firelight. "Most of them's mestizos and Yaquis. Look at their knives."

"Best we stay quiet," a slender man agreed. He relaxed against a tree, smoking a cigarette. "If they go to work on us, we won't make good buzzard bait."

"Don't cross Tafoya, not tonight," Ledbetter said. "Let him cool down."

Cotton agreed.

"I figured to be able to handle him," Bart continued. "Maybe I can still do it."

"If you don't," Vatch said, "we're in trouble." He nodded. "Real trouble."

Tafoya turned abruptly. He motioned to one of his men. "Mescal pronto." He took the bottle and uncorked it. "Senor Ledbetter." Anger hung on his words. He paused. "You said my men should not ride the trails." He drank from the bottle and snorted.

Bart nodded. "That's what I said."

"My men rode the trails and some were killed. You said you would show us the way. Is that right senor?"

He nodded.

"Then you will show us the way tonight."

"It ain't a good time. You got to be careful when you're raiding in this part of the country. Most of the ranchers know you're here and they're ready for you."

Tafoya's face twisted in frustration. "You lie!" he snarled. "You gringo liar." He turned and gestured to his men. His hand arced like a swinging knife blade. He whirled back to Ledbetter. "Gringo liar." He sputtered his rage.

Cotton came to his feet, his sixgun pointing. Ledbetter and the others scrambled to their feet. Their sixguns were weaving and ready.

Tafoya turned. His eyes flashed the anger that boiled inside. He looked at Cotton. "If you use that gun, you will not live. Muerte."

Cotton glanced around nervously. He backed away from the fire.

A Yaqui Indian moved slowly to his side, a long-bladed knife in his hand.

Cotton's eyes widened. Fear spread over his face. He slowly holstered the sixgun.

The Yaqui's knife flashed in the firelight, but he held his thrust and waved it near Cotton's throat.

Tafoya waved the Yaqui away and turned to Ledbetter. "You would be wise to put your guns away."

They reluctantly holstered their guns and waited.

Tafoya walked away and turned back. "You tell me do not raid now." He spit out his frustration. "I will guide you, you said." His eyes narrowed. "I can not trust you, gringo pig. You do not ride with us. Some of my men will ride tonight, but I will stay with you, my men and I, and wait for Billy Joe."

Ledbetter stepped toward Tafoya, but he stopped as he heard the sound of cocking guns. "What do you want with Billy Joe? He can't help you anymore'n me."

"Tonight will be glorious. We raid Senor Childress and the Matador, and I will get the gringo. I have a plan." He laughed and drank from the bottle.

"El Tigre," a Comanchero grunted.

"He is El Tigre, a son of the devil, but I will get him." Tafoya smiled briefly. He raised the mescal, drank and walked to the fire.

The Comancheros moved away from Ledbetter's fire and drifted back to their own fires, where Tafoya sat and waited with them.

Ledbetter rolled a cigarette and lighted it with a burning splinter of wood. "He's got something in mind for Billy Joe." He nodded sourly and tossed the splinter in the fire. "And it ain't good."

"I wouldn't want to be in his boots."

"We'll wait and see."

They heard the horses and looked up.

"Who is it?" Vatch glanced at Bart.

"Probably Billy Joe and Bob."

Two horsemen slowly rode into the clearing. Billy Joe and Bob dismounted and led their horses to a rope corral. They shouldered their saddles and walked to the fire.

"Senor Billy Joe." Tafoya stood and motioned with the bottle of mescal.

Billy Joe waved to Ledbetter and walked to Tafoya. "What's on your mind?"

Tafoya nodded and smiled. "Senor, you have been looking for the gringo?"

He tilted his head and studied Tafoya. A thin smile broke the hard lines in his face. "You can say that."

"He was here."

"Where is he now?"

"Gone." Tafoya handed the mescal to Billy Joe.

He raised the bottle and, as he lowered it, looked at the Comanchero. "You let him go?"

Tafoya shrugged. "I know where he is."

"Where?"

"We will go together and find him."

"Where is he? I want him." Billy Joe turned and walked to Ledbetter's fire. He lowered the saddle, paused and considered that Tafoya was not at the fire. He turned, studied the raider chief and looked at Ledbetter.

"Sit down. I want to talk." Bart shifted his position.

Tafoya walked to the fire and watched Ledbetter cautiously.

"What do you want to talk about?"

"You and—" Bart looked up at Tafoya. He could see the threat in the Comanchero's eyes. "Later."

"What the hell is it?"

Bart turned his face away and studied the fire.

"Something's wrong." Billy Joe stood, stretched the soreness from his back and looked at the Comanchero. "You said we'd get the drifter. Where is he?"

"I will show you."

"Bart," Billy Joe glanced down at Ledbetter, "you were going to tell me something."

Tafoya's Comancheros gathered in a circle around Ledbetter's fire.

"Don't prod," Bart snapped.

"You tell me or I'm riding out of here." He lifted his saddle and turned.

"Tafoya, don't—" Bart was interrupted by Tafoya's curse.

Ledbetter was caught from behind and held. A mestizo swung his carbine. Its barrel crushed Bart's nose.

He sagged back and doubled himself into a ball as two of the Comancheros began to kick him.

Billy Joe whirled and drew his sixgun. He chopped at a Yaqui Indian and stepped over him. The Indian grunted and rolled to his feet.

Billy Joe vanished into the darkness before the raiders discovered that he was gone.

Tafoya cursed and motioned the Yaqui after Billy Joe. Others followed the Indian. The sounds of running and their yelps of pursuit filled the night.

Bob tried to reach his horse and failed. He was dragged to the fire and tied.

Ledbetter sat by the fire nursing his broken nose as the Indians dragged Billy Joe to the fire. He looked at the beaten man and shook his head. "This sure ain't your day."

Tafoya walked to the fire as Billy Joe's hands and feet were tied. "Buenos dias, Senor Billy Joe." His smile became a leer. "You should not run. I am your amigo." He laughed. "Don't you trust me?"

"What are you going to do?" He struggled to sit.

"The gringo, he wants you."

Billy Joe laughed. "I guess he does."

"I have a plan, and I will take you to him." He spread his hands and smiled. "You will be safe, amigo."

Billy Joe's laugh ended abruptly. He looked at Tafoya in disbelief. "He'll kill me." He looked quickly at Bart. "Do something," he pleaded.

Bart shrugged and looked way as two Comancheros roughly lifted Billy Joe like a sack of grain and laid him across the saddle of his horse.

"Bart! Help," he begged.

As they lashed Billy Joe to his saddle, Tafoya walked to his Comancheros who were mounted. He waved them out of the clearing.

"*Vaya con Dios*," he called.

The Yaquis and mestizos gave a series of yelps

and spurred their horses out of the clearing.

Rance's eyes snapped open, and he saw the raftered roof of the shanty. The old mattress he had slept on smelled musty and damp. He remembered. It's Missus Laura's shanty. I got here last night, but I should have slept longer. Something woke me. He cautiously looked around. I was too tired to wake up this early.

The weak light of an early dawn brightened the room, and he rolled to his feet. "Oh!" he gasped as the burning pain of the knife wound rippled through his body.

"I bandaged it with black salve, but maybe it hasn't scabbed over yet," he complained.

He carefully eased his boots on and rose to his feet, moved to the window and studied the clearing. Across the scattered patches of dead weeds and dried grass, he could see the shed where he had hidden his buckskin mare. She's fine where she is, he decided. Everything seems all right, but what woke me up?

Over the early morning sounds of birds and the yelping bark of a gray fox, he heard a sound.

Tall weeds, dry to the touch, were brushed. They sounded crumpled and broken. A board clattered against the shanty side.

Maybe a fox, he thought, and maybe a Comanchero. Easing the door open, Rance drew his .44. The door creaked and groaned. He was startled by the sound and crouch-ran away from the shanty, dodged and turned to face the sound.

The hunkered shape of a man swung his gun to point. He paused, raised his head and laughed.

"Rance. Rance Long Roper." He stood, lowered his gun and, as Rance watched him suspiciously, stepped away from the shanty wall.

"Slim!" Rance relaxed and straightened. "Damn me. I thought you were a Comanchero."

"I wasn't sure it was you," he answered, "but I thought you were around."

"How'd you figure I was in the shanty?"

"The door was open yesterday when we had that set-to with Tafoya."

Rance grinned. "Where are you headed?"

"Here. I've got a little news that you should know. Last night we got to Childress's place with Joe, and Childress sure got upset. He was ready to ride then, but we talked him into waiting till Frank and me could get some of the Matador men. I came here and Frank took the others to meet Childress."

"I'll be needing some help." He cautiously turned and scanned the clearing. "Tafoya's bringing Billy Joe here, and then he's going to leave the country, he says."

"Fat chance of that happening."

"He was real anxious to help. I don't think he'll leave the country, but I figure he'll do something."

"Where'd you meet him?"

"I slipped into the camp looking for Billy Joe. He wasn't there but Tafoya was. I had to get him away from the others to talk to him. He took a little convincing, but we had a talk."

Slim listened as Rance continued. "The trails are too narrow and winding for a lot of riders. I figure

162

he'll come with about ten men."

"Ten on each trail would be more like it."

Rance nodded and studied the clearing. Long shadows of the morning sun concealed litter and junk around the corral. He turned back to Slim. "Is Childress coming here?"

"Maybe later. They're heading for Ledbetter's camp, and we sent a man to Garvey's. They'll meet him at Ledbetter's or Tule."

"The Comancheros are at Ledbetter's, unless they've decided to raid."

"Or come here." Slim raised and settled his gunbelt. "You should scout this place. It's big."

They walked up the hillside past Laura's grave. Rance turned and looked at the clearing. "This would make a pretty nice ranch." He turned back. "Let's get our horses. I want to see where that trail goes." He tilted his head at a trail that followed the ridge.

Slim grunted his agreement. "Childress ownes it now. She owed him some money on a loan. Maybe you can make a deal with him."

"I'll think on it."

The trail followed a ridge that ran back of the store and shanties, and it was covered by a dense stand of mesquite and scrub cedar that hid the clearing from them.

Rance reined to a stop where the trees thinned out around a boulder. "This looks good." He pointed. "You can see the trail and the clearing."

"It's in carbine range," Slim added. "If I set up here and they try anything, I can make it hot for them." He pointed down to the clearing and trails that ended at the clearing.

"Can they get into the clearing on the other trails?"

"They'd have a long ride to do it."

"What about this trail?"

"I don't know."

"If they sneaked up here—"

"Hell, I'd be here."

"And you'd be dead."

Slim twisted and studied the trail that wandered aimlessly along the ridge. His grin was weak. "I'll have to watch it."

"I don't know if Tafoya'll be here, but if he does come, you keep a watch on that trail."

Slim nodded and began to roll a cigarette.

Rance fingered his pocket for tobacco and papers, paused and pointed. "There's something or someone on the trail just this side of the ravine that runs south."

"Looks like two riders."

As they watched, two riders slowed and stopped near the clearing. One man dismounted and eased himself up the trail to the edge of the clearing.

"Who do you think they are?" Slim tilted his head and studied the riders.

"Comancheros?"

"Seems so to me. All the cowboys around here would ride into the clearing like they owned it."

The man returned to his partner and mounted. They nudged their horses into a walk, reined up at the corral, and surveyed the clearing.

"They're checking the place," Slim said quietly. "They'll look at the shanties and the store, then signal if anyone's with them."

Rance nodded.

As they watched, the riders moved to the shanties, the store, the ravine and returned to the corral. One rider shrugged out of his serape, and he began waving it like a flag.

16

"They're coming." Slim nudged Rance and pointed.

Where the trees merged into a morning haze, a faint line of riders followed the trail.

"I've got a strong feeling about some of Tafoya's Comancheros coming on this trail." Rance crushed his cigarette on a rock. "I don't like it."

"Don't worry," Slim answered. "I'll let you know if they do. Tafoya'll have enough men to keep you busy without worrying about this trail." He fingered cartridges from his gunbelt and filled the magazine of his carbine.

"I'd better get down to the clearing. He'll be there soon, and I want to be ready for him."

The line of riders slowed until one of the two early arrivals waved them into the clearing.

The first four riders spurred their horses into a gallop, circled the clearing and waited by the corral. They stood in their saddles and cautiously scanned the shanties and the hill beyond. The rain-packed earth had loosened under their horses' hoofs and it drifted in the air.

Tafoya led his men into the clearing. They waited beside the corral.

Rance could see Billy Joe and Bob tied to their saddles. Billy Joe rocked with his horse and sagged across the saddle, head on one side and his legs on the other. Bob glumly sat in his saddle, hands tied to the horn. It seems right, he thought, settling with Billy Joe where he had killed Laura.

Tafoya impatiently rode away from his men and looked around. He waved his arm. "Senor!" His voice echoed. "Senor, we are here."

Rance nudged his buckskin out of the trees and walked her down the hillside until he was in the open. He unbooted the carbine and butted it against his leg.

The Comancheros watched and, as he slowed and stopped, walked their horses toward him. They rode easy but held their carbines ready.

He waved them back.

"*Alto. No bueno.*" Tafoya motioned the men back and rode to meet Rance. "Senor," he called. "We talk."

"That's close enough," Rance ordered. "You can dump Billy Joe and Bob over by the store and start riding."

"They are by the corral." He gestured at the two men. "What do you have to trade? They are valuable, and I do not give them away." His teeth flashed into a smile.

"I don't trade. I don't care what you want or think. I've got no feelings for you, and what you do in Tule Canyon is your business. You said you'd bring them to me, and you kept your promise." He jacked a cartridge into the chamber and settled the carbine on his leg. "Now, you just ride on out."

"What are they worth to you?" he insisted, relaxed back against the cantle of his saddle and smiled broadly. His eyes moved up along the ridge and back to Rance. "You will perhaps not steal my horses or kill my men?"

"I just want Billy Joe and he's worth killing you for." He had slowly lowered the carbine and leveled it at Tafoya. "What are they worth to you?" The cocking hammer was loud. "With you dead, we wouldn't have any need to worry about raids, and Billy Joe's over there waiting to be killed."

Tafoya's eyes widened momentarily and his smile vanished.

"Tell your men to move Billy Joe and Bob over by the store, and then all of you go back down that trail." Rance motioned with the carbine. "I don't want to kill you, but I will if you give me a reason."

"Senor, do not push me," he blustered.

"Only if you don't move." Rance gestured with his head. "There's a man up on that ridge with a rifle. He can hit anything in this clearing." Rance's voice hardened. "Tell them to move. Now! Pronto!"

Tafoya straightened, glanced up at the trail and swiveled in his saddle. His shoulders sagged. "Sanchez!" He waved. "The gringos pronto."

Sanchez spurred his horse out of the crowd of waiting riders and led Billy Joe and Bob's horses to the corner of the store building.

"All right," Rance said. "Get everybody back down on that trail and keep riding."

Tafoya glowered at Rance and turned as Sanchez untied Bob and Billy Joe.

Sanchez roughly pulled Bob from his saddle and

wheeled his horse as he grasped Billy Joe's booted feet.

Pulled from his saddle, Billy Joe's body cartwheeled and bounced on the rain-hardened earth. Sanchez jumped his horse back to the corral as Billy Joe moved groggily and sat up.

Tafoya called to his men and motioned them to the trail. He glanced up at the ridge and his face reflected the disappointment he felt.

The Comancheros milled their horses uneasily as they watched their chief.

"Pronto." Tafoya motioned.

Rance watched the Comacheros as they reluctantly nudged their horses toward the trail and dutifully filed out of the clearing.

Tafoya looked up at the ridge and shrugged.

Rance motioned with the carbine. "Now, let's go over to the store slow and easy."

He shook his head in frustration. "I go with my men. You have the gringos."

"Not till we get to the store, then you can leave."

"No, senor. I change my mind. I stay here," he said grimly and looked up at the ridge. His eyes brightened and a smile creased his face. "You stay here and my grand Comancheros will not ride in shame."

Rance looked at Tafoya curiously. "What—"

A single carbine shot echoed across the clearing.

He glanced up at the ridge and back at the Comanchero.

Tafoya smiled. "Senor gringo, you are my prisoner." He laughed, turned and called to his men.

Rance reined up as a volley of shots rippled across

the clearing.

A series of high-pitched yelps of pursuit and the rumbling sound of running horses drowned the gunfire.

"Damn!" Rance wheeled the buckskin and spurred her into a run up the hillside. "I've got a better chance in the trees with Slim."

Slim's horse appeared on the trail racing around a large boulder. Hunkered over his saddle, he swayed wildly but clung to the horn of his saddle.

Yaquis and mestizos pounded their horses in close pursuit of Slim.

He straightened momentarily and reined his horse toward Rance and Tafoya.

Tafoya's Comancheros jumped their horses back into the clearing and spurred them into a hard gallop.

Slim's horse was terrified. Head pointed straight ahead, eyes wide with fear, it pounded toward Rance. Slim swayed in his saddle like a dead man. His horse crashed into the rump of the buckskin and continued toward Tafoya.

The buckskin wheeled but kept her feet as Rance watched Slim and his horse.

Tafoya's men raced toward him as Slim's horse crashed solidly into the Comanchero.

The horses rolled into a tangle of hoofs and men. Slim was thrown to the side where he lay unmoving.

Tafoya was caught in the tangle of horses. They rolled over the surprised Comanchero.

Dust swirled in the clearing, Comancheros collided with each other as they tried to help Tafoya, and Rance could hear his angry curses.

He lay his spurs on the flanks of his mare into a jumping race across the yard.

The Comancheros ran their horses to the pile up to rescue Tafoya.

Rance raced his buckskin onto the trail. Some of the Comancheros discovered his escape, wheeled their horses and followed him out of the clearing.

A Comanchero guard watching their backtrail straightened in his saddle as Rance leaned into his buckskin's racing turn and pounded toward the guard.

He swung his carbine like a club and felt the jarring crush of its barrel against the guard's face.

He cartwheeled out of his saddle as Rance spurred the buckskin by him.

Yaquis and mestizos followed Rance on the trail as it twisted along the floor of the ravine.

They're gaining, he thought. I'll cut through the first ravine, and if I can get to the ridge fast enough, I'll be able to hold them in the ravine. I've got too much weight on the mare to try to race them. He glanced back at his pursuers. If I stay on this trail, they'll catch me.

The Comancheros formed a tight group as they gained on Rance's buckskin.

If Laura was right, he thought, the rattlesnakes will be out in that ravine. They should keep the raiders busy.

The trail dropped down, and he hard-reined the buckskin into the ravine, jumped her between rocks and boulders and around a house-high boulder. The trail angled up the side of the ravine. Small rocks and pebbles, dust and rock chips where thrown into the air by his mare's hoofs.

He heard the Comanchero's carbines, and their ricochets spraying him with rock chips. Leading Tafoya's Comancheros, the Yaquis pounded into the ravine as Rance jumped his mare over the ridge. Unbooting the carbine as he swung his leg over the cantle, Rance dropped to the trail. He slid and bounced against a mesquite and scrambled back to the trail as the lead Comanchero spurred his horse up the ravine side.

Rance's carbine pointed and recoiled. As the raider spilled out of his saddle, he settled back of a boulder and fired at the other riders on the trail. They reined their horses to a stop in the ravine, and Rance began levering the carbine.

Smoke swirled in the air. It hung in layers and in rolling clouds of burned, acrid gunsmoke. Horses wheeled and reared in fear as their riders tried to control them.

Mestizos and Yaquis dismounted and crouched behind the boulders for shelter.

As he watched, Rance saw a large rattler sluggishly work its way around a boulder that edged the trail. Smaller snakes began moving. The sounds disturbed them and they moved toward the noise.

A man screamed. High-pitched and filled with raw fear, the cry was wrenched from the throat of a swarthy mestizo.

The firing stopped. They suddenly smelled the mustiness of the rattlesnakes.

A breech-clothed Yaqui legged into his saddle and wheeled his horse. Others scrambled to their horses. The Yaqui's horse reared and fell back. He fell and rolled across a heavy bodied rattler that struck.

Ignoring Rance's carbine, the Comancheros scrambled and ran out of the ravine.

Firing at the retreating raiders, Rance saw his bullets throw up puffs of dust as they ricocheted.

He relaxed, raised the carbine and began to reload. Sort of like old Sam Houston at San Jacinto, he thought. Tafoya, he decided, boogered me out of Billy Joe. He sighed. I'll try again. He won't go back to Ledbetter's camp, that's for sure. Maybe he'll go see Anson.

17

The Matador cowboys rode into Childress's ranch yard and dismounted. Jess Crowder broke away from the group and walked to the ranch house, where a light glowed in the kitchen. As he climbed the steps to a wide porch, Childress opened the door and stepped onto the porch.

"What took you so long?" he growled.

"Slim and Frank got to the ranch only four hours ago," he argued. "It took time to get here."

"You coulda come sooner. We ain't got much time," Childress grunted. He rubbed the palms of his hands on his pants and studied the Matador cowboys. "I see Frank, but where's Slim? He's a good man."

"He figured that Rance might need some help and he went to find him."

"Good." He turned, opened the door, and called to his wife. "We're going now. Back as soon as we can." He paused and turned back. "Abe's at the bunkhouse, and if you need help, the boys I'm not taking will be in soon." He turned to Jess. "You left some cowboys at the Matador to protect it if we miss finding the Comancheros, didn't you?"

Jess nodded. "Where are your riders?" He walked beside Childress and glanced at the empty corral.

"They're at a line camp on the way." He looked at Jess and the false dawn that was lighting the eastern sky. "Bill said that Frank was winged."

"He was, but he's patched up enough to ride."

"That's what we're going to do. If you figure like me, we'll teach them a lesson."

"I can't agree more. I sent a man to Garvey's. They'll come up the trail from Yellow House and maybe trap them."

Childress reined up on the Adobe Walls Trail and turned to Jess. "With my men and yours, we're big enough to tie a knot in Tafoya's tail."

"We'll have to do that, or if he doesn't clean us out this time, he'll be back next year." His face drew down. "We've got enough trouble with rustlers and Indians without having Tafoya and his Comancheros to worry about."

Childress nodded. "I figure we'll spread out on the trail, not too far apart, and if we run into his men we can try to box them in. If that doesn't work, we'll figure something else."

The cowboys agreed.

"Frank, you and Jess keep me company back here. Bill, you ride up ahead and keep your eyes peeled. Give us a sign when you see them."

Bill wheeled away and cantered along the trail ahead of the others.

"Do you think they'll be on this trail?" Frank unbooted his carbine and checked the loads.

"It'd be the natural thing to do. They used it when Carver was burned out, and if they're planning a raid, it's the only trail that'll handle a large herd."

"Figures," Jess said and settled back in his saddle.

"Then we'll wait and ride," Frank said quietly. He fished tobacco and papers from his pocket and began to roll a cigarette.

A hawk drifted across the ridges and ravines, and, in the distance, a vulture slowly circled.

They heard muffled sounds of a running horse.

Bill rounded a turn in the trail and slowed as he neared the three men.

"Did you see them?" Childress asked.

"There's a hell of a bunch of them."

"Comancheros?"

"I didn't ask, but they sure look like the raiders."

Jess grinned as Frank sourly looked up the trail and jacked a cartridge into the chamber.

"Bill," Childress glanced along the trail, "take about ten men and slip them into clearings up a ways. Don't do anything until we start the fight. We'll wait here and let them come to us."

"Why don't I go with Bill? I'll let them spot me and hightail it back here." Jess lifted his carbine and cocked it. "I'll bring them in like bears after a honey tree."

"Good. The rest of you," Childress directed, "get settled back of the trees and wait for us to start the fight."

They nodded and moved along the trail to small clearings and behind bushy growing mesquite.

Childress waited on the trail with Frank. They sat

their horses, and Frank rolled a cigarette. He lighted it and inhaled deeply. "Jess should be showing soon, or we can figure something is wrong."

Childress nodded, tilted his head and listened. "I hear a horse."

"Jess?"

"Should be."

Jess rounded the turn, his horse running flat out. Rain-crusted dust on the trail broke into clods of dirt that spun in the air behind his running horse. He slowed as he neared Childress and reined to a stop. "Bill was right. There's a godawful lot of them. They saw me and they're—"

Childress looked up as the hard running sound of the Comancheros interrupted Jess. "Get ready! Hold your fire till they get closer."

Frank swung to the ground and led his horse to the side. He dallied the reins to a tree limb, returned and stood in the center of the trail.

Childress and Jess swung down and moved their horses to the trees as Frank watched.

The Comancheros discovered the three men. A Yaqui gave a high-pitched yelp and fired his carbine. His bullet splashed dust near Frank.

"Not yet," Childress ordered.

A volley of rifle shots rolled their sounds along the trail. Bullets richocheted away.

"Wait till the first rider gets to the broken mesquite," Childress ordered. *"Now!"*

The three men fired.

A rider's horse reared.

Frank began to lever his carbine. Jess added to the quick shots as gunsmoke rolled and swirled.

A Comanchero's horse squealed, fell back on its rump and rolled. Its rider's boot caught in his stirrup, and the horse rolled on him.

Three raiders were hit. One fell under the closely packed horses. He screamed.

Dust began to swirl on the trail as the Comancheros's horses fearfully jumped, their hoofs chewing at the trail.

The Matador and Childress's cowboys began firing from clearings that lined the trail.

Comancheros caught in the crossfire panicked and wheeled their horses to escape. They looked into the guns of the Matador men.

Two Matador cowboys moved onto the trail from a clearing, and fired at the confused mass of Comancheros who realized the trap they were in.

Terror laid spurs to the flanks of their mustangs. They lashed their horses' rumps and charged out of the trap. The frightened horses tried to dodge the cowboys.

The Matador men waited and fired, and they were caught under the churning hoofs of the raiders' horses.

Suddenly the trail was empty. A few raiders moaned, but the two Matador men lay still.

"I want two men to clean up here," Childress ordered. "We're going to chase them all the way to Tule." He nodded to the Matador men. "Take good care of them."

"Watch the clearings," Frank warned. "They could trap us just as easy as we did them."

"Not if we stay on their tails."

"Eyahaa!" Jess's yelled rolled across the hills as the cowboys charged after the retreating raiders.

178

18

Rance reined his mare along the winding trail that
worked up through a break in the rimrock. His eyes
restlessly watched the trail, cliffs and low buttes.
The way Tafoya treated Billy Joe and Bob, I don't
think they'll go back to the camp. It seems to me
they'd go back to Anson's place. He's their pa.
There's no other place they can go around here.

A mule deer broke from its cover, dodged around a
clump of mesquite and disappeared in a gully.

He grinned. This is the prettiest country I've
seen. I'm going to talk to Mr. Childress about
buying Laura's place.

As he pushed his buckskin into a canter, a red-
winged hawk soared along a rimrock and down the
hillside. I should be able to see Anson's place from
up here, he thought. He cautiously studied his
backtrail and the rimrock, and as he moved through
a break in the rimrock, Rance slowed.

The trail led across a small mesalike plateau, and
he reined to a stop where it dropped to the flat
below. Stepping out of his saddle, Rance settled on a
boulder and studied the clearing and Anson's
shanty ranch that lay below the rimrock.

It looks like Anson's alone, he decided. There's

only one horse in his corral, unless he's got visitors and their horses are at that dry camp where he stashed me until it was dark.

He legged himself into the saddle, nudged the buckskin into a walk and allowed her to follow the trail without reins. Just in case, he thought, Rance checked the loads in his sixgun and carbine. He relaxed in the saddle and cautiously searched the rimrock and the clearing ahead of him.

His buckskin worked through the mesquite and into the clearing, where he kicked her into a canter. Circling the corral, he reined to a stop at the corner of a sagging porch. His eyes searched the clutter of Anson's yard and the clearing for signs of Billy Joe and Bob.

"Anson!" Rance legged himself out of the saddle and stalked stiff-legged to the steps. "Hello!" He knocked on a broken railing. "Anybody home?"

The door opened slightly and the muzzle of a Henry rifle threaded through the opening followed by the grizzled face of Anson. "Who be you?"

"Rance Long Roper, Mr. Canutt." He pushed his hat back. "Remember me?"

Anson walked onto the porch. "I remember you. Sit." He pointed to the edge of the porch. "I'm hearing stories about you trying to kill my boys." He glared down at Rance and hitched his pants up.

Rance carefully rolled a cigarette, pinched the end and lighted it. "I can't deny that. Billy Joe killed Laura, and it ain't right that he should go free." He raised his eyes to a trail that vanished into a ravine where a jack rabbit hopped into the clearing to catch the sun.

180

"It won't bring Laura back, killing him like you're figuring."

"What'd done is done," Rance agreed, "but Missus Laura was a hell of a good woman. She treated me like people. She saved my life and died for it. He killed her and I figure that Billy Joe's got to cotton up to me for that."

"You'll have to face me if you kill him." He glanced away and back to Rance.

"I sure don't want that." Rance stood and walked to the corner of the shanty, studied the clearing and returned.

"There ain't nobody here, if that's what's worrying you."

"They might ride in."

"They ain't been here more'n a week." He glanced away. His lips agreed. "More'n a week."

"Do you think they might show up?"

"They might." A smile tugged at his mouth.

Rance watched him from the corner of his eye. "I've got a feeling that you're not talking straight." He shifted his body and watched Anson.

"Are you calling me a liar?" Anson suddenly straightened and glared at Rance.

"I sure wouldn't do that. It's just that things don't seem right." He stood and walked to the corner. He knew, before he saw them, that Bob and Billy Joe were waiting, and he swayed back.

Billy Joe's sixgun exploded in his face.

The bullet burned a crease in his scalp, and his hat flipped into the air. Bright lights slashed at his brain. He couldn't see, but by instinct, he drew his sixgun and began firing.

He heard Billy Joe and Bob curse as they scrambled to the rear corner of the shanty.

Rance leaned against the shanty wall and raised a hand to his eyes. Blind! It's happened to others, he knew. His face felt sticky. He could see light and smiled with relief as he backed around the shanty corner, squatted and wiped the blood from his eyes with a bandana.

"They're going to get you," Anson called. He slipped through the door and Rance could hear his crazy laugh. "They're going to get you."

He wrapped the bandana around his head to slow the bleeding. They don't know that I've got a Smith and Wesson, he thought. Two cartridges hadn't been fired, and he reloaded the fired chambers. He smiled grimly. I don't like the idea of killing either of them here, but I don't have any choice. Billy Joe's here and I'm not letting him get away.

The afternoon sun threw the tall lanky shadow of Bob across the yard.

Rance carefully watched the shadow. If he thinks I've emptied the gun, Billy Joe will probably step into the open. Hunkering down, he watched the shanty corner across the porch, fired two fast shots into the ground then pointed the .44 to where he knew Billy Joe would be.

"Bob," Billy Joe called, "sounds like he used up his bullets."

"I counted five."

"Then I'm going to kill me a drifter."

Blood began seeping through the bandana, but Rance held his .44 pointed at the corner and waited.

A warm rivulet of blood ran to the corner of his

eye. He blinked to keep it out of his eye and wiped with a finger.

Billy Joe stepped into the open.

Rance squeezed.

His bullet ripped the wall by Billy Joe's head. It ricocheted, wood splinters spun in the air, and pieces of lead cut his face.

Rance wiped his eye and fired a wasted shot.

Billy Joe had ducked away.

Rance straightened, stepped onto the porch and walked quickly to the door. He watched the corner for Billy Joe as he opened the door and slipped into a darkened room.

Anson sat a table littered with mouldy biscuits and spilled bean soup. "They're going to kill you." He laughed. "If they don't, I will."

Rance ignored Anson's threat as he watched the window and backed across the room.

Anson curiously watched him cross the room until he stood beside the old man.

Rance pointed the .44 at the old man. "Give me your gun, I'm not taking a chance with you."

"No."

"Then I'll take it. I don't have time to mess around." His hand dropped to Anson's side and came up with a battered Remington cap and ball.

"Damn you," he growled, "leave that alone. You ain't got no right to take that." He angrily reached for the gun.

"I need it." Rance turned away and strode across the room to the Henry rifle, where it leaned against the wall. He took the rifle and catwalked to the window.

Anson stood up and moved around the table. "You ain't supposed to be in here. They said for me to keep you out," he complained. "They'll kill you." He raised his arms and shook them. "You get out. You get out of my house right now."

A noise by the window spun Rance around, and as he swung the .44 to point, his head exploded with a flash of light. He sagged to his knees, struggled to stand, but sprawled on the floor.

19

Consciousness slowly returned, Rance hesitantly raised his head. His eyes wouldn't open. He could feel the caked blood that held them closed. It had drawn his skin and he could taste its heavy sourness. He let his head sag and tried to remember what had happened.

"Bob," Billy Joe called, "he's coming to."

Rance forced his eyes open. Clots of blood clung to his eyelashes and blurred his sight. His head hung down and he could see a pant leg that was torn up the side. He tried to move his arms, but they were tied to something. Smoke rolled and swirled in the yard, and he could smell the wood smoke in his nostrils. He took a deep breath and raised his head.

Billy Joe's stocky body materialized in the smoke as he walked toward Rance. "They say your name's Long Roper. It'd be right if maybe we'd rope drag you or hang you for a tall tree." He laughed and turned to his brother. "But we've got other ideas."

Bob materialized beside Billy Joe and grinned. "We sure do. Now that pa and the shack's gone, we've got some ideas and you're one of them."

Rance twisted to look at Anson's shanty. He was

tied to a railing of the corral and sitting on the ground. Pain slashed through his body. He paused, turned his head and saw the shanty in flames.

"Pretty, ain't it?" Billy Joe asked.

Rance moved his mouth to speak through cracked lips. His voice was a croak.

"Trouble talking?" Bob laughed. "Pa worked you over with a stove poker."

"Where is he?" Rance forced the question.

"In the shanty." Billy Joe tilted his head. "He was afraid we'd kill him and started shooting. So we did kill him, but we saved your life." His laugh was twisted. It ended on a high note without humor.

"You killed your pa?"

He nodded and grinned. "We saved your life."

"Ain't that nice of us?" Bob started to roll a cigarette and paused. "You ought to thank us." He rolled the cigarette and lighted it. "Billy Joe," he turned to his brother. "It don't seem like he appreciates the fact that we saved his life."

Rance grimly watched the two brothers. I'm in a mess, he thought. Anson must have beat me with that poker I saw by the stove. He felt groggy and shook his head. Pain slashed along his neck and back.

"I feel insulted that you don't appreciate what we done," Bob said in mock seriousness. He leaned forward and took Rance's hair, pulled his head up and spit in his face. "No appreciation at all."

Billy Joe had squatted beside Rance. He twisted his body. "Ain't you ashamed?" His hand doubled into a fist that crashed into Rance's face. "You should apologize to Bob." His fist came back, and he

186

threw his weight into a second blow.

Rance felt his nose flatten and his head slam against the railing. He lunged at Billy Joe, the railing held, but his anger spilled from his mouth in a cry of fury.

"That ain't nice," Billy Joe said. His fist opened a wide cut in Rance's forehead.

His eyes flashed the fury he felt, and his hands strained against the ropes that held them.

"You sure don't want to cooperate," Bob sighed. "I guess Billy Joe's idea is the best."

"Good." Billy Joe stood. "It's a couple of hours south of here. We're going to teach you a lesson, and just so you'll know it ain't healthy to try to escape." His booted foot swung back and forward into Rance's face.

He felt the spur buckle rip the side of his face from jaw to ear. He remembered nothing after the lights exploded in his brain.

The easy rocking away of his buckskin slowly returned Rance to consciousness, and he opened his eyes. The stabbing pain was gone. It had changed to a pulsing agony that laced through his body. His shirt was caked with his blood. A sleeve had been torn off, and one of his pant legs was torn knee to cuff.

His buckskin jumped up a rise in the trail, his body swayed, and agony racked him. A gasp of pain escaped his lips. Rance could see the stocky bodied Billy Joe ahead. Holding his head down, Rance watched the trail. Let them think I'm still unconscious, he decided. I don't know what they're planning, but it's not good. His body stiffened when he heard Bob's voice on the trail behind him. They'll probably kill me, he decided.

"Billy Joe, I think our guest has come to."

"Just in time. The camp's up ahead and we won't have to wait for him to wake up."

Billy Joe reined his horse around a boulder and into a small clearing. Bob and Rance followed on their horses into a rock-littered area.

As Billy Joe untied Rance's feet, Bob roughly pulled him out of his saddle.

Rance stumbled and tripped. He tried to stand and his foot was kicked from under him.

Billy Joe turned to Bob. "We won't have to wait till morning. There's enough light now."

"I'll see how it looks." Bob nudged his horse across the clearing and into a steep-sided ravine.

A foul musty odor hung in the clearing. The horses attempted to pull against their dallied reins and whinnied nervously.

"Do you know where we are?" Billy Joe leered as he turned to Rance.

"Rattlesnakes?"

"That's right. Me'n Bob wondered a lot of times how long a man could live in a ravine with five dens. It's late in the season, but they're still out."

Rance felt his body recoil from the idea. "Not that!" He struggled to his feet.

Billy Joe kicked.

Rance felt his leg knocked from under him and a boot crash into his side. He gasped in pain and doubled up.

"You stay there till we're ready," Billy Joe warned. He took a rope from his saddle and started tying Rance's booted feet.

Bob returned from the ravine as Billy Joe finished. "The big one's out getting the last sun, and there's a hell of a lot of others around. Just as many as i the summer."

"ꓔood. You're mounted. I'll toss him up back of you, and you can take him into the ravine. His feet are tied with my rope. After you dump him, bring the end out to the mouth of the ravine, so we can pull him out after they've hit him."

"You're loco. I'm not going into that ravine."

"They can't get to you."

"My horse won't go in. You try it on your dun." Bob swung to the ground. "I couldn't get him closer'n twenty feet of the ravine."

"Damn it. All right, I'll take him in." Billy Joe stepped into his saddle and took Rance's body as he was slung over the dun's rump.

Bob watched as Billy Joe spurred his reluctant dun into the ravine. It whinnied nervously and, as Rance's body slid off, whirled and galloped out. Billy Joe cursed when Rance's body dropped to the trail.

Rance lay unmoving as he listened to the whirr of high-pitched rattles and the low pulsing sounds of death.

A heavy, sweet mustiness hung in the air. It seemed to suffocate him. The rattlers moved sluggishly as the afternoon cooled. They were reluctant to move, but the days were cooling, den time was near and they were edgy.

The rattlers will use this trail going to their dens, he thought. I won't get out of here alive if I don't do something fast.

He slowly inched his hands between his legs until he felt the knot. Easy, he cautioned himself. I don't want Billy Joe or the rattlers to see any movement. The rattlers'll be over here soon enough. He suddenly grinned hopefully when he felt the coils of rope. Billy Joe forgot to take the rope end back to the mouth of the ravine. His fingers moved fast as he worked at the knot. His body chilled when he heard the quiet rustling of snakes as they moved.

A big rattler worked its way down the hillside toward Rance. Its head, as large as a jack rabbit, moved around a boulder. Its emotionless eyes watched Rance, and its tongue probed the air, testing it for a victim.

The knot slipped. Rance breathed a sigh.

The big rattler slid onto the trail and swung its head toward him. It weaved just above the trail, eyes holding on Rance, as it moved along the trail.

He came to his feet and backed away from the rattlesnake. He heard Billy Joe yell, and a sudden whirring spun him around.

Two rattlers warned him off the trail.

"Get him, dammit!" Frustration edged Billy Joe's voice.

"I ain't going in there."

"Then get up on the ridge."

A bullet ricocheted from the boulder, Rance crouched and worked his way around the side of the boulder. He checked the ground around his booted feet and hunkered down to loosen the rope around his wrists.

The whirring grew louder as the rattlers sensed danger.

They're all over, he thought. He came to his feet and eased his way along the back of the boulder. Billy Joe can't get at me here, but Bob can from the ridge. Rance looked down at his hand holding the coiled rope. He laughed. "I didn't even know I had this rope. Maybe it'll help," he told himself.

A small rattler moved away from the boulder near his feet and started toward the trail. He stepped aside to let it pass.

The rattler was in no hurry and half coiled for a moment before moving on.

Bob appeared above him on the ridge and began firing.

Bullets sprayed Rance with rock chips.

He reached down for the small rattler, grasped its tail and threw in a jerking motion.

The rattler sailed up in twisting arc and landed near Bob's feet.

His yell was startled and filled with uncontrolled fear that paralyzed him. He fell back and scrambled away.

"I can't see him," Billy Joe called. "You get him."

"There's rattlers all over here."

Rance scrambled up the ridge side and crouched beneath a lip of the ridge.

A pair of rattlers below him worked their way downhill, and he could hear Bob carefully searching for him.

Bob leaned over the ridge lip and saw Rance. His first bullet ricocheted away.

Rance twisted, drew his hand back and threw the coiled rope.

Bob whirled at the swishing sound. His eyes widened when he saw what seemed to be snakes. The coils of rope fell on him. He gasped a yell, stepped back and stumbled.

Rance clawed his way over the ridge lip and scrambled to his feet.

Bob caught his balance as Rance lunged for him. He tried to chop with the sixgun, but it slipped and fell.

Rance's pent-up fury erupted in an angry roar that slammed his fist into Bob's gut.

Bob reeled back, tripped and fell over the ridge lip.

Frozen with fascination, Rance watched Bob roll, slide and bounce into the ravine.

Two rattlers struck but they missed.

The big rattler struck and held.

Bob screamed and rolled away.

A second and third rattler struck at the terrified man.

"Bob!" Billy Joe's agonized cry echoed in the ravine. "Bob! No!"

Rance slowly turned and picked up the sixgun Bob had dropped. It was Rance's Smith and Wesson. He smiled grimly and checked the loads.

Billy Joe watched in fascination as Bob contorted his body in fear.

Covered with his own blood that was caked, his clothing torn and hanging in shreds, Rance looked like a man from hell as he walked to a point on the ridge where he could see Billy Joe.

"Billy Joe!" He held the .44 at half-cock, his arm

192

hanging to his side.

Billy Joe raised his carbine and paused.

"It's just you and me," Rance called. "I'm coming down."

Billy Joe whirled, frantically swung into his saddle and spurred the dun into a hard run.

20

Childress reined to a stop and turned in his saddle. He watched Garvey and Jess slow and stop beside him.

"The turn off to Laura's is up ahead." Childress pointed. "The best I can figure is that we chased about sixty Comancheros all the way up Tule Canyon to the Panhandle."

Garvey smiled and laughed. "They really fell apart when me and my boys caught them on the Yellow House Trail."

Frank laughed. "Rance and Slim would have liked that."

"That reminds me." Garvey turned to Frank. "I'm going to have to tell Sue about Rance. Where is he?"

Frank shook his head. "No one's seen him since the fight yesterday."

"And no one's seen Tafoya," Childress interrupted. "Ledbetter's camp was empty." He turned to Jess. "Did you check the whole camp?"

"I sure did. There was a fire that was dying and we checked all over, but we couldn't find a sign of anyone."

"They may have a trail to another clearing."

"It was dark in the clearing, and we could have missed it."

"Well," Garvey sighed, "I'll have to tell her to wait."

"The fact that we didn't find Tafoya worries me." Childress scratched his chin.

"Do you think he's got the rest of his men on a raid?" Frank looked at the trail and glumly began to roll a cigarette.

"Most of the men are on the Panhandle," Childress answered. "I don't think he's in any condition to raid."

"I'd sure like to see Rance." Garvey settled himself in his saddle.

"I don't think anyone'll see him till he settles with Billy Joe," Frank answered.

"It's getting late, and we've got to get back to the Matador." Jess lifted his reins and looked at Childress. "Unless there's something you want."

Childress shook his head absentmindedly. He turned to Garvey. "If you go by Laura's place, you might look around." He cleared hs throat and spit. "If he's been hurt, send us word."

"I thought I would."

Rance kicked his buckskin into a run along the trail to the remains of Anson's shanty ranch. Billy Joe had vanished in the distance. "He's running now," Rance told himself. "Somewhere he's going to have to stop."

The burned shell of Anson's shanty still

smouldered. A thin curl of smoke drifted in the breeze, and Anson's horse raised its head as Rance took the trail to Laura's clearing.

He sadly looked at the charred remains. "Anson didn't ask for much. He didn't deserve being killed by his own boy." Rance returned his attention to the trail and watched the tracks of Billy Joe's dun horse. "He's still beating it toward Laura's. There's only one place he can go." Rance continued to study the trail.

Mesquite and scrub cedar were scant on the hills where they clumped in sporadic spots. A mule deer sneaked up the hill then broke into a run when it saw Rance.

He ignored the deer. His eyes held on the tracks that the dun horse left. "Ledbetter's camp is the only place he can go." He slowed the mare and looked closely at a cluster of boulders that edged the trail. "Bushwhack!" He reined to a stop and waited. Slowly dismounting, Rance unbooted his carbine and scrambled up a long sloping hill where he carefully studied the boulders.

I'd better check it, he thought, and he crouch walked toward the clump of boulders.

A sparrow hopped from one rock to the next, paused and watched a jack rabbit sitting beside a boulder to absorb the sun's warmth.

He cautiously edged toward the boulders and shook his head. Rabbits are dumb critters. You can't always know if anyone's around. As he neared the boulders, Rance straightened and walked to them.

Only the broken limb of a mesquite lay in the

crevasse between the boulders.

It would have been a good place for a bushwhack, he thought.

Bart Ledbetter sat by the small fire and watched Tafoya and four of his men beside a second fire. He glanced to the side as Cotton Resor grunted a complaint.

"I'm getting sick and tired of sitting here watching Tafoya. Why don't you kick him out?"

"He's got four mestizos with touchy fingers. If we make a sudden move, they'll start shooting."

"I guess you're right." He rolled and lighted a cigarette.

"Ever since they rode in after Long Roper boogered them, he's sat there like a bump on a log."

"Why don't they pack up and go to Tule Canyon?"

"He probably figures the ranchers are out riding the trails."

"They may be doing just that."

"I don't think so."

Tafoya raised his head, looked at Bart and called. "Senor Ledbetter?"

"Yeah?"

"We talk?"

Bart nodded.

Tafoya stood and walked to Bart's fire. His four Comancheros followed and spread out.

"No!" Bart motioned. "You keep your men over at that fire," he ordered.

Tafoya turned and gestured to his men. They

reluctantly returned to their fire and watched cautiously.

"My senora was right." He shook his head. "Bad," he sighed. "The trails, do you think they are clear? We wish to go to Tule Canyon."

"They're all right."

"You would not play tricks?" He studied Bart suspiciously.

"I don't play tricks. You asked me and I told you."

"I think maybe—"

He was interrupted by the sounds of a horse on the trail.

The four Comancheros whirled and backed to the edge of the clearing. They anxiously watched Tafoya for a sign of what they should do.

Bart stood and waited beside him.

A dun horse walked into the clearing and Billy Joe dismounted. He dropped the reins and walked slowly to the fire.

"Where's Bob?"

"Dead," he said bluntly.

"What happened?"

"None of your goddamn business," he snapped. "That damn Long Roper is behind me."

"The gringo?" Tafoya swiveled and studied the trail. "A guard, we need a guard."

"If you want a guard, send one of your men," Bart growled. "Long Roper knows the game trail, and a guard would be wasted."

"The sun is setting," Tafoya complained. "He can come in the dark."

"He sure can." Billy Joe turned to Bart. "You

didn't want to just let him ride out of the country. Kill him, you said. Well, you're going to have the chance.''

"We'll sure as hell do that. Cotton,'' he turned to his men, "you and Vatch drift over on the other side of the game trail and get set to wait for him. Clint, I want you down at the edge of the clearing when he comes, and Billy Joe and me'll wait by the fire to bait him in.''

Tafoya watched Bart place his men and smiled. "Are we to be bait as well?''

"No. Put your men around the edge of the clearing, and you can sit beside your fire.''

Bart watched the men settle themselves, rolled a cigarette and lighted it when he heard a horse snort.

"Roper?'' Billy Joe looked up.

Bart nodded. He drew on his cigarette and exhaled.

Rance slowed his horse and dismounted. He led her into the clearing he had used before and returned to the trail. I should be tired, he thought, but this is about over and I feel good. –

The mare snorted and shook her head.

He raised and settled his gunbelt, checked the loads in his carbine and sixgun and glanced at the trail.

It was empty, and only the hill country sounds interrupted the quiet.

"I don't hear a sound,'' he mumbled. "If there was a guard, he'd make a noise.'' He grinned. "If there isn't a guard, I'll just walk in and visit.''

Bart and Billy Joe glumly watched the fire, and Tafoya sat alone.

Rance entered the clearing and stood beside a clump of trees. He held the carbine pointed and he cocked the hammer.

"Billy Joe!"

The three men looked up.

"*Madre de Dios*!" Tafoya scrambled to his feet.

"Get him," Bart called as Billy Joe rolled away from the fire and drew his sixgun.

Rance fired. His bullet chewed at the empty space beside the fire. He crouched and slipped into the trees.

Bullets ripped at the trail. They followed Rance into the trees. Leaves clipped by the bullets fluttered to the ground. Wood splinters and bark bits spun in the air and showered down on the crouching Rance.

Clint ran from the edge of the clearing. He choked a gasp, stumbled and rolled as a Comanchero bullet ripped through his body.

"Don't shoot my men!" Bart roared, turned and shot at the man who had killed Clint. His bullet whined into a ricochet, and Bart ran to the shelter of the trees.

The Comancheros began firing at shadows. A bullet exploded the fire into a shower of live coals that fell into dried weeds and grasses.

Rance moved through the trees, watching for Billy Joe. A shadow moved and he fired, levered and fired.

Cotton Resor reeled away from a bois d'arc, stumbled and sat on the ground holding his side.

Tafoya had slipped away from the fire and waited behind a bois d'arc.

Rance slowly worked his way around the clearing, drawing a cautious shot when he made a sound. His boot broke a tree limb. It sounded loud in the clearing.

The Comancheros' bullets ripped the trees near Rance.

He moved to the side and cautiously watched the clearing.

Tafoya had been waiting. Rance backed into the Comanchero's sixgun. As he cocked his gun, Rance felt the prodding muzzle.

He whirled and swung the carbine butt.

Tafoya reeled back from the slap of the gunbutt. He tripped and fell back.

Rance squatted and, as the sixgun filled his hand, he fired.

Tafoya grunted and cried out.

The Comancheros broke from their hiding places and, as they converged on their chief, Rance backed away.

Gunfire laced the rapidly darkening clearing. He squatted and began firing as the Comancheros crouched by their chief.

The four Comancheros ran from the trees with the limp form of Tafoya, firing at any movement in the clearing.

"*Vamos pronto*," Tafoya ordered.

Rifle fire from the trees ripped at the small group. The floor of the clearing was furrowed with sprays of dirt. Ricochets whined away. A mestizo reeled and stumbled, but he followed the group.

Smoke swirled in the clearing. Weeds and grass, near the trees, were burning.

The Comancheros' horses whinnied as they were mounted and wheeled out of the clearing.

Vatch Green stepped away from his shelter and suddenly slumped as a Comanchero's bullet found a target.

The grass fire flamed up and threw crazy lights on the smoke that hung in the clearing.

"Billy Joe," Rance called.

Shots racketed in the clearing. "Go to hell." Billy Joe's voice was hoarse.

Where's Ledbetter? Rance questioned himself. He cautiously watched the tree shadows.

Bullets ripped the trees as he heard the shots from the trail behind him. He felt a bullet burn his shoulder, twisted around and fell back.

Bart appeared on the trail and loomed large as he ran toward Rance.

Rance raised and pointed the .44, thumbed and fanned three shots.

Bart's shirt was pinned against his chest. His feet twisted, his knees collapsed, as he crashed into a bois d'arc and crumpled to the ground.

Rance came to his knees.

Billy Joe appeared across the clearing.

Rance pointed and squeezed. The hammer snapped on an empty chamber.

Billy Joe laughed and walked toward Rance.

He clawed at his gunbelt for cartridges.

Billy Joe broke into a run.

Rance's fingers found only empty cartridge loops.

Billy Joe loomed larger and larger in the firelight.

Rance lifted the carbine, pointed and fired. Its barrel hit a tree limb. He missed.

Billy Joe dived to the side, twisted and fired. His bullet splintered a mesquite limb as Rance came to his feet.

He looked for Billy Joe.

A bullet ricocheted by his head as Rance began levering his carbine.

Bullets chewed at the trees.

Billy Joe sprinted across the clearing.

Rance's shots followed Billy Joe as they were levered into a barrage.

Billy Joe's churning legs stopped as a bullet ripped his body. A second bullet blew the side of his face away and exploded blood and brains into the air. He crumpled and slid into a lifeless heap.

The grass fire flickered and died.

Smoke drifted slowly in the clearing.

Rance walked to his buckskin. "It's done," he said and gently rubbed her neck. "Let's go see Mr. Childress. Maybe he's got some clothes I can borrow so I can go visit Miss Sue."

SPRINGFIELD .45-70

Springfield .45-70

John Reese

Price: $1.95 0-505-51789-2
Category: Western

Madman with a Mad Gun

Raitt was a killer with a big grudge against the world. Now he was out to get repaid for his suffering. First he'd kill rancher Mike Banterman and steal the payroll money. With his .45-70 he figured there'd be no stopping him. Power, women, money—his for the taking!

Three Complete Western Novels:

THREE COMPLETE
WESTERN NOVELS

Gun Brat
Wes Yancey

Breed Blood
Ben Jefferson

A Renegade Rides
Lee Floren

Price: $2.75 0-505-51788-4
Category: Western

Triple Western

Three action-packed, rip-roaring
adventure classics, by three of the
greatest Western writers ever to
tame the wild frontier!

Fargo #9: The Sharpshooters

John Benteen

Price: $1.75 0-505-51790-6
Category: Western

One-Man Feud

The Canfield clan, thirty strong, had left their North
Carolina mountains and were raising hell in Texas.
When one of them killed a Texas Ranger, the lawmen
sent Fargo in to root out the killer. The Rangers
wanted no quarrel with the Canfields, but they figured
Fargo was tough enough to hold his own against the
entire clan.

Day of the Scorpion
Gene Shelton

Price: $2.25 0-505-51787-6
Category: Western

The Hunter and the Hunted

The Apaches called him the Scorpion, and he was
itching to show the vicious Henderson gang the deadly
sting of revenge. The outlaws had raided his farm and
murdered his wife. Now the Scorpion had to search
the rocky desert for traces of the killers, knowing that
he couldn't rest until his wife had been avenged and
the last drop of blood had been shed.

SEND TO: **TOWER BOOKS**
P.O. Box 511, Murry Hill Station
New York, N.Y. 10156-0511

PLEASE SEND ME THE FOLLOWING TITLES:

Quantity	Book Number	Price

**IN THE EVENT THAT WE ARE OUT OF STOCK
ON ANY OF YOUR SELECTIONS, PLEASE LIST
ALTERNATE TITLES BELOW:**

	Postage/Handling I enclose	

FOR U.S. ORDERS, add 75¢ for the first book and 25¢ for each additional book to cover cost of postage and handling. Buy five or more copies and we will pay for shipping. Sorry, no. C.O.D.'s.

FOR ORDERS SENT OUTSIDE THE U.S.A., add $1.00 for the first book and 50¢ for each additional book. PAY BY foreign draft or money order drawn on a U.S. bank, payable in U.S. ($) dollars.

☐ Please send me a free catalog.

NAME_____
(Please print)

ADDRESS _____

CITY _____ **STATE** _____ **ZIP**_____
Allow Four Weeks for Delivery